BLESSINGS IN DISGUISE

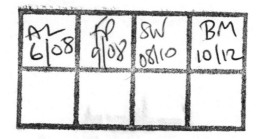

BLESSINGS IN DISGUISE

JANE MCBRIDE CHOATE

THORNDIKE
CHIVERS

This Large Print edition is published by Thorndike Press, Waterville, Maine USA and by BBC Audiobooks Ltd, Bath, England.
Thorndike Press is an imprint of Thomson Gale, a part of The Thomson Corporation.
Thorndike is a trademark and used herein under license.

The text of this Large Print edition is unabridged.
Other aspects of the book may vary from the original edition.
Set in 16 pt. Plantin.

LIBRARY OF CONGRESS CATALOGING-IN-PUBLICATION DATA

Choate, Jane McBride.
  Blessings in disguise / by Jane M. Choate.
    p. cm. (Thorndike Press large print Candlelight)
  ISBN 0-7862-8776-4 (alk. paper)
    1. Large type books. I. Title. II. Series: Thorndike Press large print Candlelight series.
PS3553.H575B55 2006
813'.54—dc22   2006009262

BRITISH LIBRARY CATALOGUING-IN-PUBLICATION DATA AVAILABLE

Published in 2006 in the U.S. by arrangement with
Jane McBride Choate.
Published in 2007 in the U.K. by arrangment with the author.

U.K. Hardcover: 978 1 405 63926 2 (Chivers Large Print)
U.K. Softcover: 978 1 405 63927 9 (Camden Large Print)

Printed in the United States of America on permanent paper
10 9 8 7 6 5 4 3 2 1

To Marcia Markland and Suzanne Rose,
who believed in me.

CHAPTER ONE

Sam Hastings's scowl deepened as he listened to the voice on the other end of the line. "Get back to me when you know more." He hung up the phone.

"What's wrong?"

He looked at Carla and felt his anger fade. Without even trying, she was able to wipe away the problems and frustrations of the day. She had that effect on him. He touched the tip of her nose and smiled. Dressed in jeans and one of his old shirts, with paint speckled on her hair and face, she shouldn't have looked so beautiful.

Her beauty had attracted him from the first; it still did, he acknowledged with an inward smile. But when he looked at her now, he saw so much more. Integrity, strength, sensitivity, compassion. It was her compassion for others that had involved him in working with the city's homeless. He sighed, his thoughts bringing him back to the problem that was holding up the construction of the community home for the city's homeless.

He helped her down from the stepladder where she'd been painting wood trim around the kitchen cabinets.

"Fowler's refusing to sell the warehouse."

When the City Council decided to sell the abandoned warehouse tentatively designated as a site for the community home to developers, Sam had used every contact he had to find a second warehouse with equally good access to public transportation, schools, and shopping. After convincing the council to use part of the profits to buy another building, he had believed the main hurdle to the project was over. Now the owner, Horace Q. Fowler, refused to sell.

Sam balled his hands at his sides. "I knew there'd be problems, but this. . . ." He shook his head. "The council's not going to like it. Not after the fire last week."

A fire had ripped through one of the upper floors of the warehouse. Structural damage had been minimal, but the resulting chaos had left several council members uneasy and ready to withdraw their support. The police had found no evidence of arson, but they hadn't ruled it out, either.

"If I didn't know better, I'd say the whole

project was jinxed."

"You'll work it out," Carla said, rubbing his cheek with the back of her hand. She looked at him and started to laugh.

"What's so funny?"

"You." She held up paint-splattered hands. "It's all right," she said between giggles. "You look cute with paint on your face."

"So do you," he said, taking her brush and swiping it down her cheek. He drew her to him, heedless of the paint that covered her. The kiss was long and deep.

It was also sweet and giving. Like Carla. Once more he was awed by this wonderful woman he'd married. Once more he was humbled by how she'd filled the emptiness of his life with her generosity and compassion. The thought brought him back to the problem of buying the warehouse, and, reluctantly, he ended the kiss. He needed to make some calls.

"Tell me," she said, wiping his cheek with a cloth.

"Fowler's stalling." Sam stabbed his fingers through his hair. "It's a fair offer. More than fair. He ought to be thanking his lucky stars that he can unload the place."

"Why is he refusing to sell?"

"Darned if I know."

"Maybe if you and I talked with him,

explained to him the purpose of the community home, he'd see how important it is and agree to sell it."

In spite of his frustration, Sam smiled. Carla always tried to believe the best of anyone, even a hardheaded businessman who was probably holding out for a better price on a rundown piece of property.

"Maybe we'll do that."

"I'd better clean up or I'll never get this paint off."

He stood back to look at her. "Oh, I don't know. I kind of like you with paint on your nose."

She swatted him with the towel.

Still smiling, Sam headed to the makeshift office he'd set up at one end of the dining room. The arrangement wasn't perfect, but it allowed him to work on his architecture business at home. That meant more time with the woman he'd made his wife just two months ago. He glanced over at Carla, who was cleaning brushes and rollers in the kitchen sink. Her dark hair was pulled haphazardly on top of her head; her lip was caught between her teeth as she concentrated on her task. She'd turned his world inside-out and upside-down. And he loved every minute of it.

No, the arrangement might not be perfect,

but it came close.

Carla awakened to the sound of the shower. She stretched lazily. It was comforting, she decided, listening to the rhythm of the water, knowing that Sam was nearby.

He was good for her in so many ways. When she started taking herself too seriously, he teased her out of it. When she needed someone to talk to, he was there. When she rushed in to solve problems, he reminded her to take things one step at a time. She smiled, remembering how he'd systematically overcome all her objections that they get married.

Her smile died as she thought about the latest problem in securing a site for the community home. Providing a home for the city's homeless had been her dream for as long as she could remember. The delay in buying the warehouse worried her more than she'd admitted to Sam. She'd been involved with enough projects to know that people — and causes — lost their momentum when they encountered a snag. It had been nothing short of a miracle that Sam had found another site. If they failed to get this warehouse, she was very much afraid that the city would postpone the building of the community home indefinitely.

She'd deliberately downplayed her worry last night. Sam had enough to deal with as the newest member of the City Council without her adding to his troubles. Differences over the community home had nearly cost them their love two months ago. She wouldn't make that same mistake again. Sam was too important to her.

"Hi, pretty lady." Sam crossed the room to bend over and brush his lips against hers.

She wound her arms around his neck. "Hi, yourself."

"Have I told you that I love you?"

"Not in the last five minutes."

He kissed her again. "I love you."

"Good." She climbed out of bed. "'Cause it's real cold out there."

"What's that got to do with my loving you?"

"Only someone really in love would run when it's this cold."

He pretended to groan. "It's freezing outside and you want to jog?"

She smiled, remembering Sam's initial aversion to her dawn runs. He'd made no secret of the fact that he wasn't a morning person. Despite his grumbling, though, he'd joined her every morning.

A mischievous light gleamed in her eyes. This time his groan was for real, and he started pulling on his sweats. He couldn't resist her when she looked at him like that.

Fifteen minutes later, his feet slapped the pavement, scattering whiffs of snow around him. "We've gotta be crazy." His words came out in short puffs in the cold morning air.

"Think what we're doing for our bodies," Carla said.

He gave her a dirty look. She was barely even breathing hard while he was struggling to catch his breath.

"I am." He grunted, wondering if he'd ever be able to feel his legs again.

Someday, Sam promised himself, he was going to outrun her. He hadn't been in such good shape in years, he admitted, but he still struggled to keep up with her.

"Slowpoke," she called over her shoulder. She jogged in place while he caught up with her.

"Enough is enough," he grumbled. He tackled her, carrying them both to the ground. He maneuvered it so that he took the brunt of the fall, and she landed on top of him.

"Oomph." The air knocked out of him, he lay there panting.

"You okay?" she asked, propping herself up on her elbows.

"Yeah."

"Good. Because that means I can do this." Before he could ask what she meant, she grabbed a handful of snow and smashed it into his face.

"Your turn now, sweetheart." Rolling so that she was pinned beneath him, he snatched up some snow and gently rubbed it in her face. The tussle left them both gasping for breath and laughing.

Her cheeks flushed with cold, snowflakes glistening in her hair; she was so lovely that his breath caught in his throat. Her hair fanned out behind her, a splash of ebony against the snow. He brushed a snowflake away, only to have it disintegrate under his touch. He touched his lips to hers, a soft caress that was in keeping with the peace of the early morning. She responded with the generosity that was so much a part of her, giving everything she had.

She shivered, and Sam realized how long they'd been lying in the snow. He stood and then offered her a hand, pulling her up and into his arms.

A mud-colored dog ran between his legs, nearly tripping him. Sam tried to catch himself but was too late. He landed with a thud.

Carla knelt down — to help him up, he

thought. He reached out his hand, only to find it ignored as she patted the dog.

"He's cold," she said, wrapping her arms around him.

Sam climbed out of the snowdrift, brushed himself off, and looked at the mutt, who resembled something between a collie and a large poodle. "He's warmer than we are. He's got a fur coat on." But he couldn't help noticing how thin the dog was beneath his fur. Sam's mouth tightened as he noticed the matted coat and unhealed sores that covered the dog's body. One look at Carla's face told him she'd recognized the signs of neglect.

"C'mon, boy," Carla murmured. "You're probably hungry, aren't you?"

The dog woofed.

They headed home, the dog running ahead then trotting back as if to say, *Why don't you two hurry up?*

Once inside, Carla found an old towel and began rubbing him dry. "Ugh," she said as the towel caught on clumps of dried mud. "You need a bath. But this will have to do for now."

When she finished, the dog caught the towel in his teeth, refusing to let go.

"Okay, you keep it," she said after a brief tussle from which he emerged the clear winner. She rummaged through the refrigerator and triumphantly produced last night's meat loaf. "Here you go, boy." She filled a plate and set it on the floor.

Securing the towel under his paw, the dog scarfed down the leftover meat loaf, then looked up inquiringly.

"You want more?" Carla asked.

Another woof confirmed her guess.

She refilled the plate. When he finished, he picked up his towel and looked at first Carla and then Sam.

"Bath time," she announced.

Before Sam realized what he was in for, he found himself wrestling a seventy-pound dog into the bathtub. Kneeling on the floor, he and Carla began scrubbing the dog. Caked-on mud turned the bathwater a murky brown. The dog squirmed and wriggled, slipping from their grasps as he chased a bubble. By now thoroughly soaked, Sam plunged his arms deeper into the water, determined to get a firm hold and not let go.

When the bathroom floor was a sea of mud-colored water, Carla pronounced the dog clean.

"Too bad we can't say the same for us," Sam said wryly, looking down at his splattered clothes.

"We'd better take him back to the park," Sam suggested after they'd thoroughly dried the dog and changed clothes. "Somebody's probably looking for him."

Carla stooped to wrap her arms around the dog's shaggy neck. "He looks like he's been on his own for weeks. Did you notice how hungry he was?"

"All the more reason to find his owner." And when they did, Sam added to himself, he'd have a talk with him about animal neglect.

She looked unconvinced. "I guess you're right."

They spent the next hour at the park asking everyone they saw about the dog. All of their inquiries met with a negative answer.

Sam knew what was coming, but he tried to head it off just the same. "We can take him to the animal shelter."

She threw him a reproachful look. "We can't just abandon him."

"We're not abandoning him. We're taking him to a place where he'll be well looked after."

"I know, we'll put up signs, advertise a lost dog in the paper. Someone's bound to claim him. In the meantime —"

Sam recognized that look. He should. He'd seen it often enough, whenever Carla decided someone — or something — needed her help. "We take him to the shelter."

"In the meantime," she said, ignoring his suggestion, "he can stay with us." She scratched the dog behind the ears. "You'd like that, wouldn't you, George?"

"George?"

"After my great uncle George. They look alike."

"Your uncle George looks like a dog?"

"Only when his hair wasn't combed. He's dead now, but I know he'd be pleased. He always liked animals. Especially dogs."

"Let me get this straight. You named your car after your grandmother and a dog after your uncle?"

"They were brother and sister."

Laughter rumbled from deep inside him, and he pulled her to him. "I love you, Mrs. Hastings."

She wound her arms around his neck. "Good. 'Cause I love you back, Mr. Hastings."

George woofed.

Laughing, Carla knelt and let him lick her face. "We said we wanted to start our family right away."

Sam sighed. "I know. I just hadn't planned

on our first baby weighing in at seventy pounds."

"He'll be gone within the week," she promised.

A week later, George had established himself as an important — and, Sam was afraid, permanent — part of the family. George had insinuated himself into their lives with a persistence that Sam could only admire. What surprised him was that he, who had never had a pet in his life, was actually growing to like George.

It wasn't that hard, Sam reflected. George was the soul of friendliness. He bounded into a room, sized up its occupants, and then jumped on the person he deemed most likely to offer him food. His only quirk was that he refused to relinquish the towel Carla had used on him that first day. It now smelled strongly of dog saliva. Attempts to wash it had met with bared teeth and bristling fur.

"Get down, you big lout," Sam said, pushing the dog off the kitchen chair. "Your bowl is over there." He pointed to where a huge plastic dish occupied a spot in front of the sink.

George gave a mournful sigh, but Sam held firm. It was bad enough that Carla spoiled the dog shamelessly. He wasn't going to fall into the same trap. He ignored a twinge when he remembered how he'd slipped George a bite of steak under the table during dinner last night. His conscience prodded him to admit the truth. It had been two bites. He had the uneasy feeling that Carla knew exactly what he'd done and was secretly laughing at him.

"C'mon," he said, pulling on George's collar.

After one more sorrowful look, George jumped down, dragging the tablecloth, complete with dishes, with him.

Sam was just finishing sweeping up the broken dishes when Carla opened the kitchen door, her arms laden with groceries.

"There you are," she said.

Sam looked up expectantly, but she was already kneeling down to pat George's head.

"I have a treat for you." She held out a plastic bone. "Now you can chew on this instead of shoes."

George pulled his lips back over his teeth. If Sam didn't know better, he'd swear the dog was smiling.

"He's never going to learn to obey if you reward him when he's done something wrong."

She ruffled George's fur. "Of course he

will. He's still a baby."

"Carla, George is seventy pounds. That's hardly a baby."

"I was speaking of his maturity, not his size. It's obvious no one's bothered to teach him any manners. That's why we have to help him learn what's acceptable. It won't take him long. He's very intelligent."

Sam sighed. He didn't hold out much hope for teaching George anything — the dog was too set in his ways — but he didn't tell Carla that. She wouldn't believe him anyway.

"No calls about George?" she asked, putting away the groceries.

Sam shook his head. He watched as she struggled to look disappointed, a smile breaking through anyway. Carla could no more hide her feelings than she could lie. Her smile had the same effect on him as it always did: It turned his insides to mush. And he knew he'd do anything to keep it there.

George chewed noisily on his bone while Carla praised him for being a good dog.

Sam resigned himself that they had a dog.

Sam read through the literature on Project Reach-out once more. For the last month he'd been searching for some way to make a difference. Together he and Carla volunteered at the homeless shelter, but he wanted — no, he needed — to feel he was helping on an individual basis.

When he'd learned about Reach-out, the brainchild of a social worker friend of Carla's, he knew he'd found what he'd been looking for. Reach-out was aimed at helping troubled youths, particularly those from the housing projects and shelters, by matching them with adult mentors.

Six months ago, he'd never have had the courage to do this, he reflected as he sat in the minuscule office the coordinator of Reach-out had managed to scrounge in the city's Parks and Recreation Center. Of course, six months ago, Carla hadn't been in his life.

"Mr. Hastings, Jared will be with you in a minute," the receptionist announced.

"Thank you."

He was annoyed to find he was nervous waiting for the boy who had been assigned to him. What did he have in common with a teenage boy? Nothing.

Sam reviewed the sketchy bit of information given to him about Jared Walker. Fifteen years old. Above average intelligence, although his school records showed his grades had slipped during the last quarter. Two minor brushes with the law, both of which had earned him a year's probation. Along with his parents, he'd lived at the shelter for the last four months. It was the last sentence that had Sam frowning. If the community home were progressing on schedule, families like Jared's would have an alternative to living in a shelter.

He forced himself to forget about the community home for the moment. Right now he had to focus on a boy who needed him.

A nervous cough alerted him that he was no longer alone. He looked up to find a lanky boy slouched in the doorway.

"Jared," the receptionist said, urging the boy forward. "This is Mr. Hastings. Mr. Hastings, Jared Walker."

Jared appeared to be all knees and elbows. Sam found himself remembering what he'd been like at fifteen. Not much different from the boy standing before him now, shuffling uneasily from one foot to the other.

Sam held out a hand. "It's Sam."

Jared looked as if he was going to ignore the gesture. Finally, he stuck out his hand. The hand was thin, too thin, the skin stretched tautly over the knuckles and wrist.

Sam tore his gaze away from Jared's hands, aware that the boy was sizing him up. They were alone now, the receptionist having discreetly vanished.

Jared gave Sam a once-over that was both defiant and frightened. He jammed his hands into the pockets of his too-short jeans. "Guess we're supposed to hang out together. Or something."

"Or something." Sam returned the look with a long one of his own.

Jared was the first to lower his gaze. "You want to do something or not?"

Under the belligerence, Sam heard the loneliness. And the fear. But he knew better than to show any sign of sympathy. He remembered enough about his teenage years to know that such an offer would be categorically rejected.

"Not unless you want to."

Jared looked as if he didn't quite know what to make of Sam's offhand attitude. "Hey, it's cool. I mean, I don't mind if we go somewhere or something."

"How 'bout we grab a burger?"

The boy shrugged into a jacket. "Yeah. I mean, that sounds good. Thanks."

Sam couldn't help noticing that the jacket sleeves fell a good four inches short of covering Jared's long arms, exposing his bony wrists. Socks peeked through holes in the black hightop sneakers. He itched to take the boy shopping and silently cursed the regulations that forbade it.

Over a hamburger, fries, and a milkshake at a fast-food place, Sam watched in amusement tinged with concern as Jared plowed his way through two deluxe cheeseburgers, a double order of fries, a fried apple pie, and a large drink.

Jared started to wipe his mouth on the back of his sleeve before picking up a paper napkin and using it. "Uh, thanks."

Sam smothered a grin. "You're welcome."

His hunger satisfied, Jared sat back and studied Sam. "How did you get hooked up with this outfit? You some kind of do-gooder or something?"

Sam thought about it. A do-gooder? Automatically he rejected the label. He remembered the words Carla had used when he'd first met her. "I'm just someone who cares."

"Why?"

The stark question caused him to frown. Because of Carla? Certainly she'd awakened him to the needs of others and sparked his desire to help them. But there was more. He'd discovered it when he helped Ethan and Maude Sandberg, an elderly couple in Carla's congregation. Giving of himself filled something inside him that he'd only recently discovered was missing.

In the end, he didn't have an answer, at least not one a teenage boy would understand. "Why not?"

Jared appeared to think about it and nodded. "You're different," he said at last.

"Different?"

"From the rest of the do-gooders who come around trying to do their thing for us poor unfortunates."

Sam winced at the scorn in the boy's voice. Fifteen was too young to sound so cynical.

"They think all they have to do is hand out some clothes, preach about the value of hard work, and they've done their Christian duty." Jared spat the last word. "I don't wanna be nobody's duty. Not now. Not ever."

"There's nothing wrong with people trying to help you," Sam said carefully.

"Yeah? You try being someone's duty. See how much you like it."

Sam couldn't help but agree as old memories came flooding back. Duty was a cold word. He ought to know. He'd been a duty to his parents for the first eighteen years of his life. He'd put an end to that as soon as he'd been able to. Impatient with his thoughts, he filed the old memories away. Right now, Jared needed a friend, not someone wallowing in the past.

"What *do* you want?"

"I want my life back!" Jared looked surprised at his outburst. "I just want my life back," he said more quietly. "It's not just me. It's Mom and Dad. They're different now. They act like strangers."

Sam searched for the right words and wished Carla were here. She'd know what to say. "Your parents are going through a bad time, but that doesn't mean they still don't love each other. Or you." He pretended not to notice when Jared knuckled away a tear.

"I wanted to quit school, go to work, help out, but Mom wouldn't let me. Said I needed an education." The last word ended on a sneer.

"She was right. You won't help them by dropping out of school."

"What good is learning algebra and French when my family is living in a shelter? If we got together some money, we'd have enough to rent an apartment. It'd be a dump, but at least it'd be ours. I wouldn't have to share a bathroom with twenty other people."

"I know it's rough, but —"

"You don't know nothing. How could you? I read up about you before you picked me up. You're some rich dude. You don't even have to work if you don't want to. You've never had to scrounge for something to eat or get kicked out of your home or wonder if you're gonna see your old man again, because you're scared he might split because he can't face things anymore."

Jared was right. "I'm sorry," Sam said quietly. "I don't know how you feel. Why don't you tell me?"

The boy looked at Sam as if trying to determine his sincerity. "You really want to know?"

"I really want to know." Sam covered Jared's hand with his own.

"Nothing's right anymore. Nothing."

Sam waited, knowing Jared needed some space. He looked at this boy-man who was caught in the middle of something no child should have to go through.

"When we lost our house, I had to switch schools. All of my friends are back in the old neighborhood. I don't have any friends now and even if I did, it's not like I can hang out with them or anything. The guy who runs the shelter has this stupid curfew where everyone's gotta be in by nine." He looked suddenly shamefaced. "I didn't mean what I said about my dad. He's the greatest. It's been hard on him, us living in the shelter and all."

Jared slipped Sam a glance. He nodded slightly, as if to himself.

"Living at the shelter stinks. But that's not the worst of it." Jared glanced at Sam before quickly turning away. "It's like I'm . . . I don't know . . . some kind of freak or something. The kids at school act like I've got some kind of disease and if they get too close to me, they might get it too."

Sam swallowed hard, praying for the right words. "You've got friends now."

"You?"

"Yeah. Me. And my wife, Carla. She's a minister. I think you'll like her."

Jared slanted him a look as if to say, *You've gotta be kidding.* "A preacher lady?"

Sam smiled. "Yeah, a preacher lady."

CHAPTER TWO

"He's just a kid. Not even old enough to drive. And he's living in the shelter because his parents can't make the rent."

Carla listened, knowing Sam needed to talk out his feelings. She'd been the same way the first time she'd come up close and personal to the problem of homelessness. She'd been sad, depressed, but most of all, she'd been angry. Angry that people were forced to live on the streets. Angry that the politicians practiced rhetoric rather than compassion. Angry that she was helpless to change it. She'd gotten through her anger only by recognizing that it didn't help. It was only then that she'd started to work to change things for the better.

One result was the shelter. It was far from perfect, but it was a reprieve for those who would otherwise find themselves on the streets. Although he didn't know it, Jared was one of the lucky ones — he and his family had found space at a shelter, space that was growing more scarce every day.

"And I take him out for a hamburger, like that's going to fix anything."

She heard the self-condemnation in Sam's voice and ached for him because of it. "You were there. You cared."

"It's not enough."

"Welcome to the club."

He smiled wryly. "Okay. I get the message. Only what am I supposed to do?"

"Exactly what you are doing. Be his friend. It sounds like he could use one."

"There's so much he needs. New clothes, shoes. But I'm not supposed to buy him anything. Some stupid guidelines that say volunteers aren't allowed to buy clothes and stuff for the kids."

"There's a reason for those guidelines," she said quietly.

He looked as if he wanted to argue.

"Without them —"

He held up a hand. "I know. I know. But when I see a kid in jeans that belong in a rag bag and a jacket that looks like his kid brother ought to be wearing it, I have a hard time remembering why I can't do something about it." He slammed his fist in his hand. "If I could just —"

She smiled.

He returned it with a sheepish one of his own. "Seems like we've had this conversation before."

"Seems like. Only the roles were reversed."

He rubbed his jaw. "How do you do it? How do you keep going back when you can't do what needs to be done?"

"How can I not?" It was no answer at all — she knew it. But it was the only one she had. It was the only one that allowed her to keep her sanity in a world where too often the only constant was overwhelming need.

He held out his arms. "I love you, preacher lady."

"Preacher lady?"

"Jared's name for you when I told him you were a minister."

She wrinkled her nose. "I'm not sure I like it."

He kissed her lightly. "All right with you if I bring Jared by tomorrow? I promised him a game of basketball and I thought we might swing by here after we're done."

Carla was pulling two loaves of banana bread from the oven the following afternoon when the kitchen door slammed open and Sam and a lanky teenager came in.

Sam laid a hand on the boy's shoulder. "Carla, meet Jared Walker."

32

Carla held out her hand. "Hi, Jared."

"Hi, Mrs. Hastings. I mean, Reverend. I mean —"

"Preacher lady?"

Jared's face reddened. He threw Sam a reproachful look. "I didn't mean anything —"

"I know," she said. "How about calling me Carla? That's what my friends call me, and I have a feeling we're going to be friends."

Jared smiled shyly. "I'd like that."

"I was just taking some banana bread out of the oven. Would you like some?"

"Sure." He looked at Sam. "That is —"

"You don't have to ask twice," Sam said. He turned to Carla. "We just finished a game of one on one. Jared's determined to make me look bad. Beat me three games out of five."

"You did all right," Jared said. "For an old —" A deep flush stained his cheeks.

Carla laughed. "For an old man?"

Jared gave a lopsided smile. "Guess that's twice now that I stuck my foot in my mouth."

"It's all right, Jared. It's been a long time since I was fifteen." Sam looped an arm around the boy's shoulders. "C'mon. I'll show you where you can wash up."

Five minutes later, they returned.

"Carla makes the best banana bread there is," Sam said, pulling out three chairs.

She cut thick slabs of bread, slathered butter on them, and poured glasses of milk. "Dig in."

After an initial hesitation, Jared devoured three pieces of bread with hardly a break. He washed them down with two glasses of milk, wiped the crumbs from his mouth, and looked up. "It was real good. Thanks . . . Carla."

"You're welcome."

At that moment, George loped in, took in the situation, and plopped his big paws on Jared's lap.

Sam started to order the animal to get down when a look from Carla stopped him.

Jared was down on his knees, wrestling with George, boy and dog rolling over each other in happy abandon. "Where did you get this great dog?"

"George sort of found us," Carla said.

Jared looked from Carla to Sam as if not quite believing his ears. "You named him George?"

Sam sighed. "It's a long story."

Jared chuckled as George licked his face. "It fits."

Carla gave Sam a triumphant look before

turning her attention back to George and Jared. She studied the two of them thoughtfully. "You know, Jared, I've been meaning to find someone to walk George. He's a big dog and needs a lot more exercise than Sam and I can give him. Would you know anyone who might be interested?"

The boy's eyes sparked with pleasure. "I'd do it. You wouldn't have to pay me or nothing."

"Of course I'd pay you."

"You mean it?"

"I mean it. You can start tomorrow if it's all right with your parents."

"Great."

"Why don't you take this home?" Carla suggested, wrapping up the rest of the still-warm bread. "Sam and I" — she searched for an excuse — "are trying to cut down on calories."

Jared looked uncertainly from her to Sam, the eagerness in his eyes plainly evident. "You're sure it's all right?"

"I'm sure," she said gently. "See you tomorrow after school, okay?"

"Yes, ma'am." He gave George one last hug.

The dog returned it by licking the boy's face again.

"It's getting pretty late. I'll run you home,

Jared," Sam said.

The smile disappeared from Jared's face completely. "It's not home. It's a shelter. They treat us like we're prisoners or something. We have to be in before nine, get up at six, can't use the shower for more than three minutes."

Carla took his hand. "Staying at a shelter is nothing to be ashamed of."

The boy jerked his hand away. "It's nothing to be proud of."

"That depends on you."

"On me?"

"That's right. You. What you think of yourself, your parents."

Jared stuck out his chin. "Hey, my parents are great. None of this is their fault."

"I know. I was just reminding you of that."

"Dad had a good job until the factory closed down last year. Then Mom got sick and had to quit her job. We couldn't make the rent and —"

Carla didn't have to hear the rest of the story. She'd heard similar ones often enough. Too often. A glance at Sam's face told her he was thinking the same thing.

"Sorry," Jared said. "I didn't mean to lay all this on you. It's just —"

"It's all right," Sam said, dropping a hand on the boy's shoulder. He checked his watch. "C'mon. I promised your mom you'd be back before six, so we'd better be pushing off."

Jared gave his lopsided smile. "Thanks for . . . everything, Carla."

"You're welcome."

In the car, Jared turned to Sam. "Carla . . . she's real nice. Pretty too. She doesn't look like a lady minister."

"What do lady ministers look like?" Sam asked, remembering his own surprise at learning that Carla was a minister.

"You know, sort of sad, like they're praying about people's sins and stuff like that."

Sam stifled a laugh, imagining Carla's reaction to the description. "I hadn't thought of it that way."

"When you told me she was a minister, I didn't know . . . I wasn't sure I was gonna like her. But she's cool." Jared lowered his voice. "I didn't know a minister could . . . you know, wear jeans. But she looked real cool in them." He glanced at Sam, a worried expression on his face. "Not that I was looking or nothing."

Sam did his best to keep his voice serious. "Never thought you were."

But Jared wasn't listening. "She gave me a job. A real job. Except it won't seem like work, not walking a great dog like George."

Sam grinned at the boy's enthusiasm.

"I wish. . . ."

"What?"

"That he was mine. We had a dog . . . before."

He didn't have to say before what.

Sam swallowed hard before closing his hand over Jared's shoulder. "Tell you what. Why don't you think George as part yours?"

"You mean it?"

"Yeah. I mean it."

"You're lucky," Jared said unexpectedly.

"Because of George?"

The boy shook his head. "Because of Carla."

Sam agreed wholeheartedly, but he was surprised that a fifteen-year-old boy understood just how fortunate he was to have Carla in his life.

Jared's next words surprised him even more. "I saw the way she looks at you."

"What way?"

"Like she . . . you know. . . ." A deep flush stained Jared's cheeks. "Like she loves you a lot." He twisted his baseball cap in his hands. "My mom used to look at my dad that way until all the trouble started. Dad used to tease her, you know, just little things. She pretended she didn't like it, but I could tell she really did. Her cheeks would get all pink, and then she'd start to laugh. I used to love to hear her laugh."

The hitch in the boy's voice tore at Sam's heart.

"She never laughs anymore."

"She's probably got a lot on her mind," Sam said, wincing at how weak his words sounded.

"Yeah. I know." Jared made a vague attempt at a smile.

Sam pulled up in front of the shelter and started to get out when Jared stopped him. "Thanks for everything, Mr. Hastings. You don't have to come in."

"It's Sam, remember?"

This time the grin was real. "Yeah. Thanks . . . Sam. See you Saturday."

Sam thought about Jared's words on the trip home. The kid was right. He was lucky. Any man who had Carla in his life would be. He experienced a rush of gratitude that she'd chosen him. Anxious to get home, he pressed down harder on the accelerator.

George was sprawled on the rug in front of the door, head resting on his front paws, when Sam walked into the kitchen. He bent down to scratch the dog behind the ears. "Looks like you're going to get more exercise, boy. Carla says you need it. But you and I know her secret, don't we?"

George jumped up, knocking Sam over and licking his face enthusiastically.

With a resigned sigh, Sam submitted to having his face washed with a rough pink tongue before picking himself up and brushing dog hairs off his wool shirt.

"What secret is that?" Carla asked, walking up behind him and slipping her arms around his waist.

He turned in her arms so that he faced her. "That you gave Jared the job of walking George because you've got the softest heart in the world."

"George does need more exercise."

Sam raised his eyebrows. George already accompanied them on their daily runs in addition to an evening walk.

"Well, it couldn't hurt him," she added defensively.

"And you figured Jared could use a job." He fitted a finger under her chin, raising her head so that their gazes were level. "Jared's right."

"Right about what?" she asked.

"He told me I was lucky."

She nodded. "Because of George. They took to each other right away."

"Uh-uh. Because of you."

"Me?"

40

"Yeah. You. He said something about the way you looked at me."

"The way I look at you?"

"The same way I look at you. The kind of look that says I love you more than anything in the world." He kissed her, long and deep. "Smart kid, huh?"

"Real smart," she said, her breathless voice doing funny things to his insides.

"He also said you were cool."

"For a preacher lady?"

"And pretty." Sam grinned. "I'm glad he's only fifteen. Otherwise I'd be feeling a little jealous."

Contrary to the doctor's predictions, Maude Sandberg, eighty something (as she liked to call herself), had fully recovered from her broken hip of a few months ago. Sam had just finished dismantling the ramps he'd installed in her house last fall for her wheelchair.

"Hope I never have to use that again," Maude said, gesturing to the wheelchair in the corner.

"You and me both," Ethan added, wrapping an arm around his wife's ample waist. "But we got through it. And we'd do it again if we had to. Just like this time." He patted Sam's shoulder. "Thanks to you."

Sam felt the color creeping up his face. "It wasn't —"

"Don't you go saying it wasn't anything," Ethan warned him. "You did us a mighty fine turn when you put those things in for my Maudie. If I couldn't have brought her home from the hospital" — his voice cracked — "I don't know what I'd have done. You saved us, boy."

"We'll never forget it," Maude added softly.

As always when he was with Maude and Ethan, Sam experienced a rush of warmth. Their love for each other wove its spell around all those who came into contact with it.

"Remember, you and Carla are coming to dinner Friday," Maude said. "I'm fixin' apple pie for dessert."

Ever since Maude had discovered that apple pie was Sam's favorite dessert, she made it whenever she invited Sam and Carla to dinner. When he'd protested that it was too much work, she'd shushed him and told him that he was family and nothing was too good for family.

The concept of family was still new to him. He'd never known the sweet feeling of belonging until Carla and then the Sandbergs had entered his life. His children, he promised himself, were going to grow up knowing they were loved and wanted, not like he had been raised, with his parents shuttling him off to boarding schools and summer camps. Nannies and later maids tended him during the rare times he spent at home.

He pushed away the old memories and grinned at Maude. "We'll be here. You know I never miss one of your meals. I've eaten at some of the best restaurants in the world, and they don't compare to your cooking."

Maude blushed. "You're flattering an old woman, but I love it."

"The truth's not flattery. And I don't see any old women around here. Do you?" he asked Ethan.

"No, sirree," Ethan said, smacking a kiss on Maude's cheek. "All I see is the girl I married sixty years ago. Still as pretty as she was the first time I laid eyes on her."

"You're both full of blarney," she said.

Sam pressed a kiss on her cheek and let himself out, still smiling.

When Carla told Maude about Jared the following day, Maude promptly included him in the invitation for dinner. Carla spent the next two days alternating between begging out of the dinner invitation and convincing herself that everything would go fine. How would Maude and Ethan take to a fifteen-year-old boy? And how would Jared react to a couple in their eighties?

I shouldn't have worried, Carla thought, watching with satisfaction as Jared put away vast quantities of Maude's meat loaf, mashed potatoes, and gravy. When Maude served deep-dish apple pie for dessert, Jared's eyes grew wide. He managed to eat two slices topped with french vanilla ice cream before declaring he was full.

"Why don't you take Samson for a walk, Jared?" Maude asked. "When you get back you can have another piece."

Samson was the Sandbergs' dog, a Christmas present from Carla and Sam. The most polite way to describe his heritage, Carla decided, was to say that he was of indeterminate breed. He looked like a dust mop with legs, which is probably why she'd fallen in love with him when she saw him at the animal shelter. She'd hoped he'd be good company for Maude and Ethan, and she'd been right.

"Thanks, Mrs. Sandberg. Everything was super." Jared bounded up from the table, nearly taking the lace cloth along with him. He gave a crooked smile. "Sorry."

"That's all right," Maude said. "Ethan's done the same thing more times than I can remember."

Ethan snorted. "Darn things. Lace and frills don't belong at a table for working men. Never did and never will. I've told Maudie that, but will she believe me?" he appealed to Sam and Jared with a shake of his head.

Carla and Sam exchanged smiles. The argument occurred on a regular basis, and was one, she suspected, that Ethan and Maude enjoyed equally.

"C'mon, Samson," Jared called. "We're out of here."

The dog yipped at his heels, clearly excited about the chance to go out.

Maude rose to start clearing the table but Sam gently pressed her back down. "It's our turn tonight."

"I'm fit as ever," she said. "I don't need any mollycoddling."

"Who's trying to mollycoddle you? I just want some time alone with my wife." He winked broadly. "I figured I'd sneak in a kiss or two while we're washing dishes. Something about all those bubbles. . . ." He let his voice trail off suggestively.

Carla swatted his arm, smiling at his foolishness.

"Come on, Maudie," Ethan said. "The young folk want to do some sparkin' in the kitchen. You and I can do ours in the parlor. Remember when I used to come courtin' and your pa sat with us in the parlor, making sure that I didn't take liberties with his little girl?" He grinned at Sam and Carla. "I managed to take a few anyway."

Maude's cheeks turned pink. "Get along with you, old man. You were a caution sixty years ago, and you haven't changed a bit. You're as shameless as ever."

"That's 'cause I married you. A man's got a right to be a caution when he marries the prettiest girl in three counties."

Maude's smile was that of a young girl as she allowed Ethan to lead her away.

Carla laughed. "Have you ever seen two people so much in love?"

"Only you and me."

She looked up, expecting to see a teasing smile on his face. But the expression in his eyes was perfectly serious. He circled the dish towel around her waist and pulled her to him. "As long as we're here, let's take advantage of the privacy." He touched his lips to hers.

When they drew apart, Carla put a shaky hand to her lips. "I like the way you do dishes." She eyed the stack of dirty plates. "But maybe we should try the old-fashioned way."

46

They spent the next half hour washing and drying the china, with its old-fashioned pattern of sprigs and flowers. Holding a plate almost reverently, she traced the delicate design of leaves and roses. "Maude told me they bought these right after they were married. Sixty years," she murmured. Carefully she began to stack the dishes in the mahogany breakfront.

"I intend on beating their record," Sam said, folding her into his arms and dropping a kiss on her cheek.

"Ah-hem."

A cough came from the doorway and they pulled apart. Carla looked up to find Maude and Ethan at the door.

"Jared's back," Maude said, looking from one to the other, her eyes sparkling with amusement. "I promised him another piece of pie." She busied herself fixing a plate with an enormous slice of pie and a scoop of ice cream.

Blushing, Carla made a production of wiping her hands on a towel. "We were . . . uh . . . just finishing up."

"It's all right," Sam said, catching Carla in his arms. "We don't mind you catching us necking. Especially since I know you and Ethan were doing the same thing in the parlor."

Muttering something about fool men, Maude bustled out with the pie. She returned within a few minutes, smiling mistily. "You know what that sweet boy said? He told me he'd never had pie this good in his life. Made me feel right good. Breaks my heart to know him and his parents have nowhere to go." She wiped away a tear with the hem of her bib apron. "You bring him with you next time you come to visit," she instructed Carla and Sam. "There's nothing I like better than having a young person around, especially one who appreciates his food."

"He's a good boy," Ethan added. "A mite on the quiet side, but that's all right. You bring him back and Maude will fatten him up. He's nothing but skin and bones."

"I can't think of a better place to take him than here," Carla said, earning a pleased smile from Maude.

Ethan shook his head. "It's a shame. A young fellow like that with no place to live but a shelter. A dern shame."

"We're working on that," Sam said with a look at Carla.

Jared wandered in then, Samson at his heels. "Thanks again, Mrs. Sandberg, for the pie. It was great."

"None of that 'Mrs. Sandberg' stuff

around here," she said. "How would you feel about calling me Grandma Maude? I know I'm not real kin, but it'd make me feel right good to have a boy like you call me Grandma. Ethan and I never had any grandchildren of our own."

"I'd like that just fine."

He blushed as Maude pressed a kiss on his cheek.

"You come back anytime, you hear?" she said. "You're family now."

"Yes, ma'am, I mean, Grandma Maude."

"They're all right," Jared said on the way home. "I mean they're sort of old and everything, but they're pretty cool."

Carla hid a smile. "You're right. They're pretty cool."

Jared threw her a sharp look. What he saw on her face must have reassured him, for he smiled. "Yeah. Mr. Sandberg asked me if I'd be willing to do some fixing up around the place for him. He said he couldn't pay much, but that's all right. He said he'd teach me how to use his tools."

"What did you tell him?"

"I said sure." He darted a worried look at Carla and Sam. "It would only be on weekends," he added hurriedly. "I'll still be able to walk George for you."

"I wasn't worried about that," Carla said,

trying not to let the concern show in her voice. Maude and Ethan lived on a fixed income, a pension Ethan had earned from his years as a factory worker. They couldn't afford to pay someone to help out around the house, no matter how small the salary. She also knew she couldn't offend them by interfering. They wanted to help Jared and were doing the only thing they could.

"It's all right, isn't it?" Jared asked. "I'll do a good job for them."

"I know you will," Carla said.

After they'd taken Jared back to the shelter, she expressed her concern to Sam. "Maude and Ethan can't afford to hire Jared."

"I know." He brushed her cheek with the back of his hand. "I think they know that too. This is their way of helping."

"I know, but —"

"Do you want to take that away from them?"

She shook her head. "How did you get so smart?"

He leaned over to kiss her. "I had a good teacher."

The red light on the answering machine was blinking as they walked in the door.

Carla rewound the tape and played the message.

"Reverend Hastings, this is Dr. Skerrit at Community General. Mrs. McCarthy is asking for you. She probably won't last much longer."

"I've got to go," she said, fishing her keys from her purse.

"I'll take you."

She shook her head. "You're exhausted, and I don't know how long I'll be."

"Call me if you need me?"

She ran the back of her hand against his cheek. "Always."

The unmistakable odor of a hospital — fear laced with antiseptic — assailed her nostrils. The combination was potent and one she knew intimately. Fluorescent lights cast harsh shadows over faded green walls. She quickly made her way to the second floor. She recognized the nurse who approached her as one who'd cared for Mrs. McCarthy in the past.

"I'm sorry, Reverend Hastings. Mrs. Mc-Carthy died an hour ago."

Blindly Carla groped for something to hold onto. The breath hissed between her teeth. For a moment the room spun around her, and she bit down hard on her lip. The pain restored her balance.

The nurse helped her to a chair. "We tried

51

calling you."

"I was out. I found the message on my answering machine."

She was too late.

Mrs. McCarthy, ninety-two and spunky, had never asked anything but that she not die alone. Carla blinked away the tears that pricked her eyes. Was she to spend her life being too late for the people who needed her? She pushed away the self-recrimination. There'd be time enough to feel sorry for herself later. Right now there were things she had to do. She started to rise.

"The arrangements —"

"I wouldn't worry about it," the nurse said kindly, easing Carla back into the chair. "The doctor contacted Mrs. McCarthy's son. He was listed as next of kin. He'll be flying in tomorrow."

"Tomorrow," Carla repeated.

She drove home in a blur. She found Sam going over a sheaf of papers, George at his feet. Sam took one look at her face and crossed the room to take her in his arms.

"Mrs. McCarthy?"

"She died before I got there. I was too late."

"You got there as soon as you got the message."

"It doesn't matter. I wasn't there for her. That's all she ever asked of me, and I failed her."

"You didn't fail her."

"How can you say that? She was all alone. No one should have to die like that."

She couldn't hold back the tears any longer. He held her as she cried until there were no tears left, only dry sobs that racked her body.

"Don't do this to yourself, Carla," Sam said gently. "You can't be there for everyone. Even if you could, you'd cut yourself up into so many pieces you wouldn't be any use to anyone."

"What good am I if I can't be there for the people who need me?"

"You were there for Ethan and Maude, the people at the shelter. You were there for George." His voice lowered. "You were there for me."

"You?"

"Don't you think I know what you did for me? You gave me back that part of myself I'd buried in a pile of work and parties."

"You did that on your own."

"Don't you believe it. It was you."

She stared at him in wonder. "You really mean that?"

"Yes. You turn yourself inside-out giving

to everybody else," he said. "When was the last time you took anything for yourself?"

The argument was a familiar one, the only real source of contention between them. Carla couldn't bring herself to be angry at Sam, though. He was concerned about her. The knowledge warmed her. It also caused her pain. She couldn't change who she was, any more than she could ask Sam to change who he was.

"If only I hadn't —"

"Hadn't what? Gone to dinner at Maude and Ethan's? Spent the evening trying to help a kid who's had more than his share of rough breaks? What would you change?"

"Nothing," she admitted.

"Then stop trying to be everything for everybody. No one can do that. Not even you." He slipped his hands beneath her hair and rubbed her neck, her shoulders, her back, kneading and stroking until she felt the tension drain out of her. She melted further into his embrace, savoring his near-ness and warmth.

"Be what you are. That's all anyone can do."

His words made sense. It was time she stopped beating herself up.

Three days later, Carla placed a single rose

on the coffin. The funeral had been a simple one, as Mrs. McCarthy had requested. After the graveside service, Ted McCarthy, her son, drew Carla aside. "I know it's short notice, but I've got to wrap everything up before I go back to Oregon. I've arranged to meet Mother's lawyer today. I'd like you to be there."

Two hours later, Carla was blinking away tears upon learning that Mrs. McCarthy had left everything to the church in her will, to be used at Carla's discretion.

Ted McCarthy pressed her hand. "Mother wanted to leave something lasting behind. You were the person she trusted to know what needed to be done."

Frowning over Sunday's sermon that evening, Carla stifled a groan when the phone rang.

"Reverend Hastings?"

"Yes." She jotted down a thought.

"Find another place for your community home."

Her attention caught, she dropped her pen. "Who is this?"

"That doesn't matter. Stay away from the warehouse and you'll stay healthy."

It didn't take much imagination to read between the lines. "But why —"

She was left with an empty dial tone. And
a knot of fear in her throat that refused to
go away.

CHAPTER THREE

"When are we taking the stuff to the shelter?"

Carla looked at Sam in surprise. "How did you know?"

"Elementary, my dear Watson." He ticked off the points on his fingers. "One, you've been stewing all week about what to do with the money Mrs. McCarthy left the church. Two, you've been chewing your fingernails more than usual today. Three, you went shopping and came home with clothes, shoes, sheets, blankets, and enough food to feed a small army. Am I right?"

"Right, Holmes. Do you think Mrs. McCarthy would be pleased?"

"I think she'd be very pleased."

"I thought about giving the money to the community home fund, but with everything up in the air and more people showing up at the shelter each night —"

"You decided the shelter needs help right

now." He grabbed her hand. "C'mon. We've got a delivery to make."

The shelter hummed with laughter, the clatter of dishes being washed, the thump of a ball bouncing on the cement floor. Carla had once marveled that those living there found it in them to still enjoy life. Now she was no longer amazed by the strength and resiliency of the human spirit. Especially those of the children.

"Sam, Carla, it's good to see you." Tom Beringer, the coordinator of the shelter, hugged Carla and shook Sam's hand.

"We brought you a few things," Carla said, handing over the first of the bags of food. "There's more in the car."

Tom gestured to the three boys playing basketball. "Jared, Tim, Rob. How 'bout you guys unload the reverend's car?"

"Sure thing," Jared said, skidding to a stop inches in front of where Carla and Sam stood.

"I'll give you a hand," Sam said, punching the boy lightly on the arm.

"That husband of yours is a miracle worker," Tom said after Sam and the boys had gone. "He's turned Jared around completely. That boy had a chip on his shoulder the size of Texas when he came here, Sam knocked it off."

Carla felt her heart swell with pride.

Tom peeked inside the bag of food and gave a low whistle. "You been out robbing banks again?"

"Not quite."

"She sounds like quite a lady," Tom said after Carla had told him about Mrs. McCarthy's bequest.

"She was."

She and Sam stayed to help stock the cupboards with the new supplies.

"Uh, Reverend?"

She turned and saw a man dressed in Army fatigues. "Yes?"

"I got something I need to tell you."

She looked at him expectantly.

"Not here." The man pointed to a back room. "There."

Carla and Sam exchanged looks before following him into a storeroom.

The man shuffled from one foot to the other. "It's about the warehouse. Word on the street is that someone with lots of juice don't want anyone messing with it. Word also is that the fire wasn't no accident."

Sam clutched the man's arm. "Who told you that?"

The man shrugged off Sam's hold. "Like I told you. The word's out." He grinned, his teeth a flash of yellow beneath a thick mustache. "We didn't exactly introduce ourselves."

Carla laid a hand on the man's arm. "If you know anything that would help . . ."

"I said, I don't know nothing more. Only . . ."

"Only what?" Sam demanded.

"Only someone's plenty mad at you and your lady."

Sam's lips tightened, and Carla slipped her hand in his. "It's just street talk," she whispered, more concerned with Sam's reaction than she was with the warning. Ever since she'd told him about the anonymous call, he'd been more protective than usual.

Sam pulled a card from his wallet and handed it to the man. "Here's my number. If you hear anything, let me know. I'll make it worth your while."

The man accepted the card. "I'll let you know. But I don't want nothing for helping her." He nodded toward Carla, "She's one of us." He gave Sam a hard look. "We help our own."

"Thank you," Carla said softly.

He nodded once more and shuffled away.

She glanced over at Sam as they finished stocking the shelves. He didn't say any more about what they'd learned, but she knew he was worried. She was concerned too. The trouble at the warehouse was a lot more serious than she'd realized.

Sam picked up Jared the following afternoon, his mind still on what he and Carla had learned at the shelter last night. Threats against himself left him unmoved; threats against Carla made him angry. But overriding the anger was fear. Gut-deep fear that Carla could become a target.

Jared slumped in the corner of the car, arms folded across his chest, eyes downcast.

"What's up?" Sam asked, heading toward Jared's favorite burger hangout.

"Nothing."

" 'Nothing' must be pretty heavy."

Jared darted a sharp look at Sam. "It's nothing you can do anything about, so can we drop it?"

"Okay."

The boy looked surprised at Sam's easy acquiescence.

It wasn't until he'd put away two double deluxe burgers, an extra-large order of fries, and a chocolate shake that Jared opened up. "It's Dad. He's real depressed."

Sam wasn't surprised. He knew Jared idolized his father. He also knew that Jared's father blamed himself that his family was forced to live in a shelter. It wasn't hard to understand Hank Walker's feelings of guilt. Given the same situation, Sam figured he'd probably feel the same way.

"Would you like me to talk with him?" he asked.

"Would you?"

"Sure." Sam wasn't sure at all, but he couldn't tell Jared that.

"You could do it when you drop me off . . . if you want. Dad was supposed to go on a job interview today, but it was called off. I guess that's why he's so down."

"Sounds good."

An hour later, Sam was regretting his hasty offer. He waited uneasily for Jared to bring his father to the shelter's small sitting room. What did he think he was doing? He was no counselor; he was an architect. He didn't have a chance to change his mind, for Jared reappeared, followed by his father.

Jared started to stammer out an introduction when Sam stopped him. "Why don't you let me and your dad get acquainted on our own for a while?"

Jared flashed him a relieved look before disappearing.

"Sam Hastings." Sam held out his hand, but the other man ignored it.

"Hank Walker."

Hank was a big man, the muscles in his arms bunching as he clenched his hands at his sides. He eyed Sam warily.

"Jared tells me you've had some rough breaks," Sam said, dropping his own hand.

"He's got no business talking about me to strangers."

"I'm not a stranger. At least not to Jared." Sam took a seat on a vinyl sofa. "I hear you're good with your hands."

"I'm fair to middlin'." Hank lowered his bulk into the room's one chair.

"I'm looking for people not afraid to work to help out at a warehouse that's going to be turned into a community home. We can't get inside yet, but there's plenty to be done outside." Sam knew he was taking a chance cleaning out the vacant lots surrounding the warehouse, but he was gambling that when Fowler saw what they'd accomplished, he'd be more willing to talk terms.

"I ain't never been afraid to work. That's how I come by these." Hank held out his hands. Calluses ridged his palms. He gave Sam a none-too-subtle scrutiny. "You look like you ain't afraid of working either."

"I put myself through school working construction in the summers." Sam held out his own hands for Hank's inspection.

The man took his time studying Sam's work-hardened hands before nodding slightly. "Jared says you're some fancy architect now."

"I design buildings."

"You didn't get those designing." Hank gestured to Sam's hands.

"I still like to swing a hammer now and then."

Once again, Hank nodded. Sam felt himself being sized up, just as Jared had done a week before.

"I don't take charity," Hank said bluntly.

"I wasn't offering it," Sam said just as bluntly. "I was offering a job."

Hank's shoulder slumped. "I've always taken care of my own. The way my pa took care of me and my brothers and sisters. Now I can't even put a roof over my boy's head."

"You're still taking care of your family. Being laid off is nothing to be ashamed of."

"I know that here." Walker pointed to his head. "But here" — he laid a hand on his heart — "I don't feel it. Not anymore. Do you know what it does to a man to see his family living in a shelter because he can't get a job? It makes him start doubting himself. Start wondering if he's worth anything. It eats away at a man until there's

64

nothing left and pretty soon he's no good to no one."

"Look, Mr. Walker, I won't say I know how you feel, because I don't. But I do know how Jared feels about you. That boy loves you."

Walker's eyes filled with tears. "He's a good boy."

"Jared's a boy to be proud of."

"You're right about that. I just wish his old man was somebody he could be proud of."

"Don't you know how much Jared worships you?" Sam asked. "He talks about you all the time. According to him, you can do anything you set your mind to."

"Yeah. His old man can do anything. Anything but find a job."

"There's one thing Jared didn't say about you."

"Yeah?"

"That you liked wallowing in self-pity."

The big man stood up and took a step toward Sam, but Sam held his ground. "You don't pull your punches, do you?" Hank asked.

"No."

"Not many men would get away with saying that to my face."

Sam thought he detected a grudging note

of admiration in the man's voice.

"Not many men care about your son the way I do. Jared needs a father, not someone who's too busy feeling sorry for himself to see that his boy needs him." Sam paused, letting his words sink in. He knew he was taking a risk of offending Jared's father, but he'd gambled that Hank was man enough to hear the truth. "I'm Jared's friend. I'd like to be yours too."

The war between pride and need was plain on Hank's face. Sam waited, knowing the man would come to a decision in his own time, his own way.

"I'd like that," he said slowly. "I'd like that real fine."

"About that warehouse job. When can you start?"

Hank grinned. "You name the place and the time. I'll be there."

Carla pulled her hair on top of her head, secured it with pins, and looked in the mirror. She scowled at what she saw there. With her hair piled in an elaborate arrangement of curls, she looked like a little girl playing dress up. She yanked the pins out, taking a few strands of hair with them. "Ouch."

Dressing for a City Council party would never be one of her favorite activities.

Tonight's party, to be held at the mayor's house, was a command performance. As the newest and youngest councilman, Sam would be on display. As his wife, she knew she would also be on display.

Her black dress was new. She was pleased with the effect of the simple yet sophisticated style, but her hair refused to cooperate to complete the image. She started the painstaking task of swirling it into curls on top of her head.

Sam crossed the room to stand behind her. He stilled her hands and began to brush her hair until it fell in soft waves about her shoulders. Lifting it aside, he dropped a kiss on the nape of her neck. "You're beautiful."

She made a face. "I'm never going to fit in with all those other women with their expensive dresses and jewels and —"

"You'll be the most beautiful woman there." The warmth in his voice banished all her doubts.

She looked at his reflection in the mirror and saw the lines of stress on his face. The worried expression in his eyes belied his light tone. Neither of them particularly enjoyed the political functions they were required to attend as part of Sam's job as city councilman, but there was something more in his eyes now.

"I met Hank Walker today."

So that was it. "What's he like?"

"A good man who's had more than his share of bad luck." He paused, remembering the rough emotion in Hank's voice when he talked about Jared. "A man who loves his son."

"What can we do to help him?"

Briefly he told her of his plan.

"You really think you can get him on the cleanup crew?" she asked.

"There's a lot of work to do outside. Heavy lifting. Hank's a natural."

"I thought those jobs were all filled."

Sam suddenly looked uncomfortable. "I've got some favors I can call in. Besides, the boss and I are . . . uh . . . close."

She had it now. "You're paying the crew, aren't you?"

"I was just trying to get things started," he said, clearly embarrassed.

"You're a fraud, Sam Hastings. You let me believe the city was footing the bill and it was you all the time."

"Guilty as charged. What's my sentence?"

"Come here." She stood on tiptoe and kissed him. "We'll save the rest of your sentence for later."

He took her hand. "Come on. We've got a party to go to."

Her groan was only part pretext. She adjusted his black tie. "Looking pretty sharp, Councilman Hastings."

He took a deep bow. "Thanks." He draped the blue scarf she'd knitted him for Christmas around his neck. "Now I'm ready."

They spent the half hour it took to drive to the mayor's house discussing Jared's family. Carla nearly forgot her nervousness, until they turned onto the private driveway leading to the estate. Lush lawns stretching in all directions, formal rose gardens flanking the sides, white columns rising up to support the four-story mansion. It all added up to one thing: money. Lots and lots of money. They were ushered inside by a white-coated doorman.

Twin chandeliers dripping with thousands of crystal prisms scattered rainbows of light across the marble floor. Flowers vied with the more potent scent of expensive perfumes. The black tuxedos of the men provided an effective foil for the dazzling dresses of the women.

Carla gripped Sam's hand more tightly before consciously forcing herself to relax. She squelched the tiny voice inside her that whispered, *You don't belong here.* It was no different than any of the other political functions she'd attended since marrying

Sam, she reminded herself. The laughter was too shrill, the voices too bright, the music too loud. Cheeks were kissed, empty compliments given, plastic smiles exchanged.

It was a game, Sam had told her often enough. A game where the stakes were higher than she ever imagined, the currency power and influence, and the players the movers and shakers of the city.

"Relax," Sam said. "It looks like there's going to be great eats." He pointed to the buffet tables groaning with an array of delicacies. A dozen tables, topped with floor-length skirts, were loaded with more food than she'd ever seen outside a restaurant.

She smiled, remembering the first such party Sam had taken her to. She'd shocked their hosts by gathering up the leftover food and taking it to the shelter. Now it was standard practice for the hostesses of the parties to urge Carla to take all the leftovers to the shelter.

"Sam, glad I caught you," a voice called.

She turned to see Pete Hammond, the senior member of the City Council, make his way toward them. He paused to clap men on the back and buss the women's cheeks. Pete was a big, blustery man with a ruddy face and the beginnings of a paunch.

"Can I steal your husband for a few minutes, Reverend Hastings?" Pete asked.

"Of course."

Sam gave her an apologetic look before allowing himself to be led away.

Left alone, Carla did what she did best at such functions. She listened. It seemed everyone had a story to tell and no one who cared enough to listen. After acting as the audience for several people, she slipped away and found an empty chair pushed against a wall. There she removed her high-heeled pumps and dug her toes into the plush Aubusson rug.

She was sighing with pleasure when Sam joined her.

"Caught you. Don't you know it's against the law to be comfortable at one of these things?" He tugged at his black tie and undid the top button of his pleated white shirt.

"I won't tell if you don't." She slipped her shoes back on. "What did Pete want?"

"Don't ask."

"Let me guess. He doesn't want the deal for the community home to go through."

"Right the first time."

She gave herself a one-minute lecture on the evils of judging others before she trusted herself enough to speak. She hadn't liked Pete Hammond from the first time she'd met him. So far, she'd seen no reason to change her opinion.

"Could he be behind the trouble at the warehouse?"

Sam frowned. "I wouldn't have thought so. But now . . ." He shrugged.

"Why does he want to stop it?"

"That part's easy. He belongs to an investment group. They've had their eye on the building for a long time, just waiting for the owner to indicate an interest in selling."

"It's nothing but a rundown warehouse."

"It's not the building they're interested in. It's the land it's sitting on. That and the surrounding lots are a prime area for development. Pete's a sharp businessman with an eye out to make a buck, but I didn't think he'd stoop to anything like this."

"Didn't as in past tense?"

Sam nodded to where Pete and his wife, Barbie, were talking with the mayor. "I don't know."

Carla followed his gaze. "I can't pretend I like the man, but I hope you're right about him not being involved."

"So do I. I don't much like his politics, but I've always believed he was honest." Deep furrows scored Sam's forehead. "He's pretty ruthless in getting what he goes after, but that's not a crime. What worries me is some of the other council members are starting to withdraw their support as well. They think we'd be better off looking for another location or dropping the idea all together."

She swallowed her disappointment. Finding another location meant even more delays. "Can't they see what the community home will mean to people? Can't they —" She suppressed a groan. "Barbie's coming this way."

Barbie Hammond threaded her way through the crowd, pausing here and there to shake hands with other guests.

Carla fixed her smile in place as Barbie kissed both her cheeks.

"Sam, Carla, how lovely to see you here."

Carla held out her hand. "Barbie. You look wonderful."

It was true. The older woman was radiant, from the crown of her silver frosted hair to the tips of her silver evening shoes.

Barbie preened, smoothing her hands over her hips.

"Thanks. I had to diet for a month to get in this dress. But it was worth it."

Carla groaned inwardly and hoped Barbie wouldn't get started on her grapefruit diet again. She'd heard enough about it at the last party to last her a lifetime.

Barbie turned her thousand-watt smile on Sam. "Sam, you don't mind if Carla and I have a little girl talk, do you?"

He looked at Carla, who pressed his hand reassuringly. "I'll see you a little later," he said.

Barbie waited until Sam was out of earshot. "Husbands. We love them, but sometimes it's nice for us girls to talk by ourselves, isn't it?" She gave a just-between-us smile that invited Carla to join in her amusement.

Carla made a noncommittal reply and waited. Barbie hadn't cornered her for some girl talk. People like Barbie Hammond didn't do anything without a reason.

Barbie's smile grew sly. "Pete tells me Sam is surprising everyone with his . . . uh . . . progressive views."

Now it was coming. "Progressive views?"

Barbie waved her hands. "You know, this community home thing."

"Wanting a decent place for people to live can hardly be called progressive."

"What would you call it, dear?" Barbie asked.

"Compassionate."

Barbie looked nonplussed. But only for a

74

moment. "Well, of course, we all feel sorry for those people. I know I just shudder whenever I think of people living in those horrid shelters."

"They're not horrid," Carla said quietly. "But they're not a home either."

"Of course. Of course." Barbie tapped scarlet-tipped nails against her jeweled evening bag. "You know, Pete can be a big help to Sam on the council."

"Oh?"

The mask fell from Barbie's face. Suddenly she was no longer beautiful. Her eyes were cold and hard, her mouth pinched and tight. "Come off it, Carla. I'll grant you that you've got the naive little minister act down pat. But you know the score as well as I do. You convince Sam to back down from the community home project and I'll see to it that Pete backs Sam's proposals for low-income housing." She smiled knowingly. "One hand washes the other."

"Fortunately Sam's hands aren't dirty. Now, if you'll excuse me —"

Barbie grabbed Carla's arm. "Not so fast, honey. You're making a mistake if you and your husband don't learn to play the game. A big mistake."

"I'll leave the game-playing to you, Barbie." Deliberately Carla turned her back, looking wildly about for Sam. She found him talking with the caterer.

He disengaged himself and joined her. He took one look at her face and steered her toward a corner where they could be alone. "What's wrong?"

"That woman." She took a long, steadying breath. It helped. Some.

"Barbie?"

"She just tried to strong-arm me into convincing you to drop the plan for the community home."

Sam whistled under his breath. "Pete must be more anxious than I thought." He took her hand. "Come on. Let's get out of here. I've done my duty with the mayor. And I've already made arrangements for the caterer to deliver the leftovers to the shelter."

Later that night, Sam sprawled on the bed and watched Carla brush her hair. It was one of his favorite activities. Rhythmically she pulled the brush through her dark hair, causing it to snap with electricity.

George pounced on top of him.

"Get down, you oversize baby."

George looked at him with a hurt expression in his eyes before jumping to the floor.

"I've been thinking about Barbie Hammond," Carla said, turning around to face Sam. "Do you think she could be behind the threats?"

He frowned. "Barbie's shallow, selfish, and vain, but she doesn't strike me as having the guts to carry off something like that."

"A woman will do a lot of things to help her man."

"In Barbie's case, it's more likely she would do it to help herself."

"She couldn't have set the fire by herself," Carla said, thinking aloud. "She'd have to have hired someone."

"That takes connections."

"I'll start putting out some feelers. Not much goes on that the street people don't know about."

He didn't like the idea of Carla asking questions among the people who made their homes on the streets. Those questions could get back to the wrong people, people who wouldn't hesitate to put a stop to them and to the person asking them.

"Why don't I do that?" he asked in what he hoped was a neutral tone of voice. "You've got more than enough to do already."

"And you don't?" She gave him an exasperated look. "Let's have it."

He tried to bluff it out. "What?"

"We promised we'd always be honest with each other. You don't want me asking questions, do you?"

He was silent for several minutes. "No, I don't. I don't want you getting hurt."

"And I love you for it. But nothing's going to happen to me. These people are my friends. They wouldn't do anything to hurt me."

Sam gave a defeated sigh. He'd never make Carla understand that there were men in the world who'd slit their mothers' throats for five dollars.

"Take George with you when you go out, all right?"

Her lips kicked up at the corners. "Do you see George as protection?"

"No. But the rest of the world doesn't know that he's afraid of his own shadow."

Hearing his name, George jumped on top of Sam, his tongue lolling. Sam submitted to having his face licked before the dog settled upon his chest, yawned widely, and began to snore. Sam looked over at Carla and found her struggling not to laugh.

"Go ahead. Say it."

Her laughter rippled over him in pleasant waves. "All right. I will. You spoil George just as much as I do. Probably more. I've seen you sneak pieces of meat to him underneath the table when you think I'm not looking."

"Guilty as charged." Absently he scratched George behind the ears and smiled when the dog gave a grunt of pleasure in his sleep. "He sort of grows on a person."

Carla gave him an I-told-you-so look.

George's snoring grew louder.

Carla's grin grew broader.

Sam reminded himself that the bedroom door had a lock.

Jared had lost the sullen expression in his eyes that had twisted at Carla's heart the first time she'd seen him. He now looked like a fifteen-year-old boy rather than a man who'd seen too much of the world's pain.

He greeted every outing she and Sam planned with an excitement that sparked their own enthusiasm. Skating in the park, a wienie roast outside despite the frigid temperature, and an evening spent watching old movies and eating popcorn all met with the same boyish eagerness.

What would he think about tonight's activity? she wondered. Serving coffee and sandwiches and giving out blankets to the people who made their homes on the streets wasn't most people's idea of a good time, she acknowledged. So why did she expect a teenage boy to go along? Maybe it was just wishful thinking, a desire that Jared understand there were people who needed what he had to give. She stole a glance at him. He looked like a typical teenage boy, all knees and elbows, hair a little too long, eyes glazed over as he watched television.

"You ready?" Sam called from the kitchen.

"Almost," she said. "Just getting my boots on."

George at his heels, Sam carried a box of blankets and two sacks of food into the living room. "Hey, Jared, you want to give me a hand?"

"You bet." Jared pushed himself up from where he sprawled on the sofa and took the box from Sam. He hefted the box onto his shoulder and opened the front door. "We ready?"

They looked expectantly at Carla. "Ready," she confirmed.

"Is it going to be like . . . you know . . . dangerous or something?" Jared asked as they drove to the inner city.

Carla smiled, remembering Sam's concern for her the first time he'd helped her distribute food and blankets. A glance at his face told her he was thinking the same thing.

"No. It's not dangerous. Not in the way you mean, anyway. But it can cause you to start thinking."

The boy made a face. "I do enough of that in school."

Carla quickly coughed to cover her laugh. "Not that kind of thinking."

"What kind?"

"The kind where you start thinking about someone else."

"Oh. You going to go all preacher lady on me and start lecturing me on how lucky I am and how I ought to be grateful for everything I got?"

She ignored the good-natured sarcasm. "No. I just want you to see things from a different angle."

Jared turned to Sam. "She make you do this kind of thing a lot?"

"She doesn't make me do it. I do it because I want to."

"You two are pretty weird, you know that?"

But the words, Carla noted, held no rancor, only bemusement. "Yeah. We know."

"Just don't expect me to get all weird too. I mean I don't mind going along tonight, but . . ." Jared hunched a shoulder in a typical teenage fashion.

"Don't worry, Jared," Sam said. "We don't expect you to get all weird."

"Yeah, well, just so you know."

The temperature had dropped ten degrees

in the last hour. Carla huddled deeper into her coat, grateful for its warmth. It had been a Christmas present from Sam to replace the one she'd given away a couple of months ago to a woman living on the streets. They'd made a pact that they wouldn't spend much on their gifts to each other, preferring to make a donation to the shelter. Sam had started frequenting discount stores, something he'd never done in his life, to find a coat for her and still remain in the limits they'd set. She smiled, remembering his shy pleasure in giving it to her.

She'd knitted him the blue scarf now wrapped around his neck. He wore it whenever he went out, claiming it was his good-luck charm. She recalled the wonder in his eyes when she'd presented it to him.

Giving and accepting love was still new to Sam.

Her mouth tightened as she reflected on what he'd told her of his childhood. He'd had everything a child could want, everything but love. She was teaching him that love didn't have to be earned. It was a gift, freely given.

Sam had a great capacity for love, one he had only begun to tap. She'd seen the quiet satisfaction in his eyes when he worked with the youths in her congregation. He had a special affinity for those who were troubled, something that allowed him to reach them when everything else had failed.

"We're here," Sam said, drawing her back to the present.

They spent the next hour handing out sandwiches, coffee, and blankets. People crowded around them, as eager for a warm word as they were for food.

Jared shivered and rubbed his hands together on their way home. "It must be twenty below out there," he said.

"Not quite," Carla said mildly.

Jared turned suspicious eyes first on Carla and then on Sam. "This is what you were after all along, weren't you?"

"What?"

"Showing me how good I got it. I've got something to go back to, even if it is a crummy shelter. The people out here" — he jerked his thumb toward the street — "don't even have that."

"We asked you to come with us tonight to help us give out the food and blankets. But I'll admit we had an ulterior motive." She laid her hand on Jared's.

"We wanted you to see that you have something to give."

"Yeah? What?" He squirmed in his seat to turn his pockets inside-out. "I'm loaded all right. I've got a whole two dollars on me."

"Your time. Your caring." She aimed a level look at him. "That's all we wanted."

He looked unsure. "Yeah?"

"Yeah."

Jared was subdued for the rest of the trip home. "It was different, handing out stuff to those people," he said after long moments had passed. "One kid didn't even have a coat or gloves or nothing." He looked embarrassed. "I feel different too."

Carla and Sam exchanged looks.

"How come you do it?" Jared didn't wait for an answer. "I guess you don't have much choice, do you?"

"Not much," she agreed.

"I didn't know people lived like that," Jared said. "Being at the shelter's rough and all that, but it's still *somewhere.* Why do they stay on the streets?"

She remembered Sam asking the same question months ago. "They feel they don't have anywhere else to go."

Jared slid Sam a sidelong look. "Guess I'm not so bad off after all."

"Guess not," Sam said.

They didn't talk much after that. Carla was content to let Jared think about what he'd seen tonight. She reached over to squeeze Sam's hand. He returned the gentle pressure.

"You were great with Jared tonight," he said after they'd dropped him off.

"Thanks. I hope it wasn't too much for him. It's not easy, seeing people live like that."

Sam curled his fingers around the nape of her neck, slowly massaging away the tension she hadn't even been aware of until now. He always seemed to know what she needed.

"Mmm. Don't stop."

When the phone rang, she was tempted to ignore it. She was deliciously comfortable, on the verge of drifting to sleep under the gentle ministrations of Sam's hands. Habit won out, though, and she picked it up.

"Stay away from the warehouse, preacher."

CHAPTER FOUR

"Reverend Hastings?"

"Yes."

"It's Jack Thompson. You know, Jack's Fix-it Shop?"

"Of course. How are you, Jack?"

"Not so good," came the terse answer. "Look, I can't talk right now. Could you meet me later? After I close the shop?"

"Do you want to come here?"

"No. I can't be seen with you. Maybe you could come to the shop around seven. Everyone will be gone by then."

She hesitated. After the anonymous call last night, she'd promised Sam she wouldn't go out alone at night until all this was settled.

"I wouldn't ask, but it's important. It's" — his voice lowered — "about the warehouse."

She heard the worry in Jack's voice. And something more. Fear. It convinced her. "I'll be there." Sam would understand. He had to.

"Thanks, Reverend." Jack hung up abruptly.

Still holding the phone, Carla replayed his conversation in her mind, trying to make sense of it. Only one thing was certain. Jack was afraid. She'd been acquainted with the man for three years and had never known him to be frightened of anything. But he was now.

Fifteen minutes after seven, panting heavily, she rapped on the back door of Jack's repair shop. A series of calls had made her late, and she took a minute to catch her breath. She called through the door. "Jack?"

No answer.

She tried again. "Jack, it's Reverend Hastings." The wind had picked up, and she knocked louder. "Jack. Open up." She tugged her coat more tightly around her.

The door gave way under her pounding. Cautiously she inched it open. "Jack? Are you there?"

She waited, all the while growing more nervous. "Jack? It's Carla Hastings. Please let me in."

The wind caught the door and slammed it shut, startling her. Impatient with her jitters, she tried to get her bearings in the darkness. Edging across the room, she tripped over something. She grabbed hold of the edge of a table and barely avoided falling. Groping for the light switch, she flicked it on, blinked against the white glare of the fluorescent lights, and saw what she'd tripped over.

A body.

A gasp caught in her throat. For a moment, she just stood there, unable to move. Finally she forced herself to kneel beside the inert figure, and she tugged at it until she could turn it over. "Jack!" Blood trickled from a wound at his temple. She felt for a pulse and found a faint beat.

She dialed the emergency numbers and waited for the ambulance, praying all the while. Less than ten minutes later, she was following the ambulance to the hospital. Her prayers had become a litany until the words blurred together. At the hospital, she gave the necessary information to have Jack admitted. The constant ringing of the phone at the nurses' station reminded her of the call she dreaded to make.

A few minutes later, she hung up the phone and pressed her forehead against the cool glass partition separating the waiting room from the admitting office. Jack's wife, Sylvie, had taken the news with a calm

Carla could only envy.

She looked at the phone again and knew she couldn't put off the second call any longer.

"Where are you?" Sam's voice barked over the line.

"The hospital." She heard the sharp intake of breath and hastened to assure him. "It's not what you think. I'm all right."

"How do you know what I think? I've been half out of my mind worrying about you and now you tell me you're at the hospital."

"Sam, Jack Thompson's been hurt."

"Is he going to be all right?"

"I don't know."

"I'll be there in ten minutes."

"Thanks."

She settled where she'd be sure to see Jack's wife when she came in.

A few minutes later, Sylvie arrived. She grasped Carla's hand. "Thank goodness you were there."

Carla led Sylvie to a chair and got her a cup of coffee.

A harried-looking doctor appeared just as Carla and Sylvie had started on their second cups of coffee. "Mrs. Thompson?"

Sylvie stood. "I'm Sylvie Thompson."

"Your husband's going to be all right," the

doctor said. "We want to keep him over-night, but you can take him home tomor-row."

Sylvie clutched his arm. "You're sure, Doctor? About him being all right?"

"I'm sure. You can see him now if you want. He's pretty groggy."

"Thank you. Thank you." Sylvia turned to Carla. "You go on home, Reverend. You've been here long enough."

"I'll wait," Carla said. "Sam's coming pretty soon."

"If you're sure . . . I don't mind admitting I could use the company."

"I'm sure."

"If you hadn't found him, he might be —" Sylvie's voice quivered.

"Don't, Sylvie. Don't think about it. Jack's strong. He's going to be fine."

Sylvie gave Carla a grateful smile. "Thank you. For everything." She hurried down the hall.

Carla sank onto a vinyl couch in the wait-ing area. She wasn't looking forward to Sam's reaction. He had every right to be angry. She'd been foolish. At the same time, though, she'd done the only thing she could. She could only hope he'd understand. A commotion at the nurse's station made her look up. She'd find out soon enough, she thought, seeing Sam stride toward her. Her breath jammed in her throat at the look on his face.

He crossed the room to take her in his arms. "You're all right?"

"Yeah." She gave in to the need to rest there in the safety of his embrace.

He released her just long enough that he could tilt her chin up and look at her face. "You're sure?"

She managed a wan smile. "I'm sure."

"How's Jack?"

"He'll be all right. Sylvie's here. I told her I'd wait with her."

Together they settled back on the couch. When Sylvie returned, Carla hurried to her feet. "How is he?"

Sylvie's face was lined with fatigue, but her smile told Carla everything she needed to know. "He recognized me . . . told me he loved me."

Carla hugged Sylvie. "Sounds like he got the important things right."

Sylvie insisted Carla and Sam go home. "They promised to set a cot up in Jack's room for me. I'll be fine."

"You're sure?" Carla asked.

"I'm sure." Sylvie turned to Sam. "Take her home. She's been here even longer than I have."

Much as she longed for home, Carla wasn't looking forward to the lecture she knew was coming once she and Sam were alone. He followed her in his car, giving her a breather.

"Don't you know what could have happened?" he asked once they were home. "It might have been you lying on that floor. You in the hospital with a concussion. You . . ." The shiver that snapped down his spine had nothing to do with the frigid temperature outside.

The stricken look in her eyes caused him to regret his harsh words, but he had to make her understand the risk she'd taken. He couldn't dismiss last night's warning, especially combined with the attack on Jack.

"I didn't know what else to do," she said. "Jack sounded so frightened. I couldn't get hold of you. I had to go."

"I know." Carla would always do what she felt was right. It was one of the reasons he loved her so much. "It's all right," he said, drawing her to him.

"I'm sorry," she murmured against his chest.

He crushed her to him, and she gave a tiny squeak that was half protest, half laughter. He gentled his hold, still needing to assure himself that she was here, unharmed. If anything had happened to Carla . . . He shuddered, unable to complete the thought.

He held her away from him and fitted his finger under her chin, lifting it so that their eyes met. "What happened to Jack changes things. It's not just a couple of anonymous calls anymore. Someone's playing for big stakes."

"But why? Why all this trouble over a warehouse that was abandoned in the first place?"

"That's what I'm going to find out."

"That's what *we're* going to find out."

He'd known it was coming, but there was no way he was going to back down now. Swallowing his frustration, he bit back the order that she was to stay away from the warehouse until this was over. Giving orders wasn't his style — not that Carla was likely to take them anyway. He was congratulating himself upon his good sense when his mind conjured up pictures of her lying helpless on some floor. All his good intentions vanished.

"You're staying out of this."

"I'm already in this," she pointed out. "I couldn't stay out if I wanted to. Which I don't."

"What about what I want?"

The determination in her eyes wavered. He knew he was playing dirty, but right now he didn't care. Protecting Carla was all that mattered.

"If I promise not to go out at night alone —"

He grimaced.

"Tonight was a mistake," she said.

"You got that right."

"Sam, Jack is a friend. I can't just turn my back on him because things become a little dangerous."

"A little dangerous? Jack was knocked out. It could have been worse. A lot worse." He curbed his frustration and took her hands in his. "I'm not asking you to turn your back on anyone, just to play things safe. Let me find out what's going on."

"I can help you," she said eagerly.

He kissed her forehead. "If you really mean that, you'll be careful, not take any chances. Please."

He started to name all the reasons why she should do as he said. In the end, he gave the only one that mattered. "I love you."

Her lips curved. "That's cheating."

"I know."

He felt her melt against him. His fingers tunneled through her hair as he held her.

"All right," she said. "I'll stay out of it.

For you."

The following morning, Carla visited Jack at the hospital.

"Sorry to mix you up in all this, Reverend," Jack said.

"I was mixed up in it before you called." She eyed his pale face with concern. "We don't have to do this now. We can wait until you feel —"

"I'm all right."

"You're sure?"

"I'll be a lot better when I get this said."

She folded her hands in her lap and waited.

"Someone approached me. Wanted to buy my shop. Offered a lot of money. A lot more than what it's worth." He laughed shortly. "Believe me, I was tempted. I bought it a year ago. The rent was cheap, and the neighborhood looked like it was going to turn around, but the shop's a long way from making big money. So I got to wondering why anyone would want a rundown fix-it shop. Then it occurred to me that it is located right by the warehouse. I put two and two together and started asking questions." He smiled faintly. "Sylvie always said I'm too nosy for my own good. I must have asked the wrong people. You know the rest."

"You really think the offer on your shop and the trouble at the warehouse are related?"

He shrugged. "Your guess is as good as mine. All I know is I stirred up something, but I'll be darned if I know what."

She pressed his hand. "You took a risk telling me all this, Jack. I appreciate it."

"Maybe you shouldn't be thanking me."

"Why not?"

"If whoever did this learns I told you . . ."

He didn't complete the sentence. He didn't need to.

Carla spent a few more minutes with Jack before saying good-bye. In the hospital lobby, she ran into Sylvie, who seemed inclined to talk. Carla was only half-listening, and she hoped she made the correct responses. Her mind was still reeling from Jack's conjectures. Last night she'd discounted Sam's worry over her safety. Now she wondered if she'd been too hasty. The thought left a sour taste in her mouth.

Tony Owens scowled as he read the paper's headline: *Local Store Owner Attacked.*

The boss wasn't going to like it. Tony didn't much like it either. Publicity was the last thing they needed.

It wasn't supposed to go down that way.

One little tap on the head and all heck broke loose. Cops. Ambulances. He hadn't meant to hit the guy so hard. He'd just wanted to scare him. Tony shrugged. It wasn't his fault the guy decided to spill what he knew to that nosy lady preacher. Well, it couldn't be helped.

Maybe the guy would wise up now and keep his mouth shut. Tony had grown up on the streets. The first thing you learned was when to dummy up. The second thing was where to hide when you forgot the first.

It would blow over soon enough. And if the boss got all bent out of shape, well, that was just too bad. Tony didn't take nothing from no one. He'd had enough of that from his old man. His father — he sneered at the word — had knocked him around plenty. When Tony had turned sixteen and towered over his old man by a couple of inches, he'd fixed him but good. Nobody messed with Tony now. Not if they knew what was good for them.

He thought back to the shop owner. These things happened. The boss would just have to understand.

He swallowed the last of his beer and punched out the private number. Maybe the boss hadn't read the paper today. Maybe . . .

"You fool," the voice at the other end of the line snapped.

Tony swallowed his anger. "It couldn't be helped."

"You should have taken care of things before they went this far."

"You paid me to scare the guy. That's what I did. You want something else done, you gotta pay for it." It felt good, Tony decided, being the one who called the shots for a change. Real good. He was tired of being pushed around.

"I paid you to do a job. Do it."

Tony held the phone a good ten seconds after the click signaled that the connection had been severed. His lips tightened. Someday he was going to pay back the boss for treating him like dirt. His scowl faded as an idea occurred to him. Someday might come sooner than he thought.

A meeting with Horace Q. Fowler had seemed like a good idea two days ago when Carla had set it up. Sitting in his office now, she wasn't so sure. She flipped through the pages of a year-old magazine, wondering what she could say to the man to convince him to sell his warehouse to the city.

"Reverend Hastings."

Carla stood as Sarah Barclay, Fowler's

personal secretary, bustled into the reception room. "I'm afraid it's going to be a little while longer. Mr. Fowler's running behind schedule."

Sarah was comfortably padded and grandmotherly looking, with hair more gray than brown. She looked like a plump little sparrow, Carla decided, with her serviceable tweed skirt and beige sweater set.

Carla sank back into the vinyl upholstered chair and looked around. The waiting room was as nondescript as Sarah.

"It hasn't been a good day. Mr. Fowler's not in the best of moods," the secretary whispered conspiratorially. "Would you like some coffee?"

"Yes, please."

An hour later, Carla was still waiting. Was the man deliberately putting her off? The thought rankled. If that was his plan, she'd simply outwait him.

An intercom buzzed. Sarah coughed slightly. "Mr. Fowler will see you now."

Collecting her purse and files, Carla stood. "Thank you, Ms. Barclay."

"Please, make it Sarah." The older woman squeezed Carla's hand. "I just know we're going to be friends."

Carla smiled. She had at least one ally here.

Fowler's office was a surprise. Considering the man's reputation as a successful businessman, she'd expected plush carpets, heavy mahogany furniture, maybe a piece or two of original art on the walls. Instead, the office was plain, almost spartan, with a cheap carpet on the floor, a strictly utilitarian desk, and two chairs. The walls were bare.

Horace Fowler made no attempt to stand. Head bent, he appeared to study some papers. At last he looked up and checked his watch. "You have fifteen minutes in which to state your business, Ms. Hastings." His smile was thin, more a quirk of the lips than a real smile.

It chilled her even as she forced an answering smile to her own lips. "Reverend Hastings."

He nodded. "Reverend Hastings." Again, that smile.

She schooled herself not to flinch. "Mr. Fowler, thank you for seeing me."

"Fourteen minutes."

She wanted to rip the watch from his wrist. Instead, she smiled again. "About the warehouse —"

"Ah, yes." He tented his fingers over his chest. "The warehouse."

"We're anxious that the sale go through as

100

quickly as possible. You see, we plan to build the community home —"

"I'm not selling."

She ignored that. "There are people living on the streets right now. Do you have any idea what that means? Do you know what it's like to sleep in a doorway, go through garbage cans looking for something to eat — not for yourself, but for your children? We need the community home. And that means we need your warehouse." She realized she was bent over the desk, fists clenched, voice verging on shrill. She took a deliberate breath and leaned back, ordering herself to relax. She wouldn't get anywhere this way.

"Do you always become so emotional when discussing business, Reverend Hastings?"

Feeling her temper threatening to flare again, Carla made a valiant effort to rein it in. Her smile once more fixed in place, she said, "Mr. Fowler, if you could just try to understand what this means to so many people, I'm sure you'd see your way clear to sell."

His upper lip stretched into what she supposed was another version of his smile.

A shiver chased down her spine. *Stop it,* she ordered herself. He was a respectable businessman. There was no reason for her uneasiness.

"I'm sure your husband didn't go into all the details with you concerning the ins and outs of selling the warehouse, Reverend Hastings. Husbands often don't with their wives." He gestured vaguely with his hands. "Women often get emotional and don't understand matters of business. Such things are better left to men to ponder."

She bristled at the implication that she was of subhuman intelligence, but she kept her smile intact. "What are you trying to say?"

"Only what I said before. I'm not selling."

"What would it take to convince you to change your mind?"

Her hopes soared at the speculative look in his eyes, only to die at his next words. "Things like this take time," he said ponderously. "Studies must be made. Opinions sought." He spread his hands.

Carla considered giving him an opinion. "When do you think these studies can be completed and opinions found?"

"In time. In time." He checked his watch. "You have two minutes remaining. Is there anything else you wish to discuss?"

She shook her head, afraid to trust herself to speak.

"In that case, please close the door behind you." He bent over a sheaf of papers, signaling that the interview was over.

Once more in the outer office, she snatched up her coat, fuming all the while.

"Bad interview?" Sarah asked sympathetically, putting a cup of coffee in Carla's hand.

Carla nodded and sipped the coffee gratefully. It was heavily laced with sugar, too sweet for her taste, but it warmed the cold spot the meeting with Fowler had left with her.

"I'm sure he didn't mean to offend you," the secretary said. "If I thought it would help, I'd speak to him about the warehouse for you."

Carla managed a wan smile. "That's very kind of you, but I don't want you to jeopardize your job."

"Oh, I don't think there's much danger of that. I've been with Horace for twenty years." Sarah laughed lightly. "He couldn't get along without me, and he knows it."

"I'm sure he couldn't."

Sarah patted Carla's hand. "You just let me know if there's anything I can do to help you."

"Thank you. You've been very helpful."

"The man's impossible," she told Sam when she returned home an hour later. "He actually timed our meeting. And all he said when I asked him about the community home was, 'Things like this take time.' I wanted to punch him out."

Sam struggled not to laugh. The idea of Carla punching out anyone . . . He couldn't help it. A laugh broke through despite his good intentions.

She glared at him. "It's not funny."

"I know." Another laugh escaped, and he clapped a hand over his mouth.

Her glare intensified.

He waited, knowing she couldn't be angry with him — with anyone — for very long. It simply wasn't in her.

"All right, maybe I'm overreacting."

"Just a little," he agreed.

"But that doesn't change the fact that the man is a —"

He bit back another laugh. Carla didn't believe in swearing, so she was occasionally forced to invent names for people who didn't share her commitment to helping others. Obviously her imagination had failed her when it came to Mr. Horace Q. Fowler.

"Not a very nice person," she finished.

Sam folded her into his arms, resting his chin on top of her head, and inhaled the citrus scent of her shampoo. "I think that pretty well covers it."

"Good. Now what are we going to do about it?"

"About changing Mr. Fowler into a nice person?"

She snorted. "I guess we could wait for a miracle to happen, but I'm not going to hold my breath for this one. I was thinking maybe we could find out why he doesn't want to sell. If we could figure that out, we might know how to convince him."

"Makes sense."

"I'm going to do some digging."

He didn't like the sound of that. He liked the innocent expression in her eyes even less. In his experience, that look promised trouble. "What kind of digging?"

"Just a little research at the public library. Maybe the hall of records. Find out the history of the warehouse."

"Fowler's owned it for the past twenty years."

"Since Sarah's been with him," she murmured.

"Who's Sarah?"

"His secretary. She offered to speak to him about the warehouse for us, but I couldn't let her do that. A man like Fowler would probably fire her for insubordination or something. I'll be back before dinner." She smiled up at him. "It's your night to cook."

He resisted the urge to squirm at the reminder. "How about I take you out?"

"Uh-uh. You promised me your famous lasagna. I'm holding you to it."

"Uh, Carla?"

She turned to him expectantly.

"I may have exaggerated about my lasagna. It's not all that famous."

"Just how famous is it?"

"Hardly at all," he admitted with a sheepish look.

Arms folded across her chest, she fixed him with a stern gaze. "Sam Hastings, have you or have you not ever made lasagna before?"

"Does heating up a microwave dinner count?"

"No."

"Then I guess the answer's no."

She surprised him by reaching up to brush her lips against his. "I'm glad."

"You are?"

"Sure." She kissed him again. "If you were perfect, I'd have to repent my feelings about Mr. Horace Q. Fowler. I'm giving myself two more days to be angry with him."

"Then what?"

"Then I'm going to kill him with kindness."

Sam was still laughing when she closed

the door behind her.

Her research trip was an exercise in frustration. After hours poring over old records, she turned to the microfilm section. They yielded no better results than the more current records. It wasn't that she couldn't find what she was looking for. What she was looking for didn't exist. She smiled ruefully, wondering what she'd expected. A story that the warehouse had once been the hideout of a gang of bank robbers who'd stashed their loot there? The site of a murder with a body buried somewhere beneath the floor?

The warehouse had no nefarious history. It was simply what it appeared to be: an empty warehouse whose usefulness had outlived its life.

Then why was Fowler resisting selling it?

Carla returned home, more baffled than ever. She found a note on the kitchen table saying Sam had gone to the office. She smiled at the lopsided heart with their initials penned inside.

When the phone rang, she snatched it up.

"Carla?" She heard Sam's smothered yawn. "Sorry, sweetheart. I'm going to be late."

"You're just trying to weasel out of making lasagna."

He chuckled. "You've got me nailed. Give me a rain check?"

"As long as that's all it is."

"I got a call and I have to meet someone."

"What about?"

"I'll tell you when I get home. Don't wait dinner for me. I don't know how late I'll be."

"It's all right," she said, stifling her disappointment. "George and I will keep each other company."

"I'll be home as soon as I can."

"I know."

She hung up the phone, feeling oddly restless. She didn't feel like cooking just for herself, so she settled for cold cuts and a salad. Switching on the television, she flipped through the channels. Even her favorite detective show failed to hold her interest tonight, and she turned off the set after a few minutes. George wandered in, crossed the room, and rubbed his head against her legs.

"You miss Sam too, don't you, boy?" she asked. "I know, why don't we surprise him with gingerbread when he gets home?"

George woofed loudly and wagged his tail.

"All right," she said, bending down to pat him. "You can lick the bowl."

In the short time they'd had George, she'd

learned that he had a sweet tooth, especially for gingerbread, which just happened to be Sam's favorite as well. George now put his paws on her shoulders, knocked her over from her squatting position, and plopped on top of her. He took a swipe at her face with his tongue. With seventy-odd pounds centered on her chest, she could scarcely breathe.

"George, get off me before I suffocate."

George gave her face a final lick before removing himself.

The homey tasks of measuring, sifting, and mixing the ingredients eased her loneliness. She slid the pan into the oven and offered the bowl to George, who licked it eagerly. Soon a spicy aroma filled the kitchen. She looked with resignation at the pile of dirty dishes.

Washing up wasn't nearly as much fun without Sam, she decided. Smiling, she remembered the first time he'd helped her with the dishes. Sam had spent the evening with her while she'd been baby-sitting for members of her congregation. He'd even helped her change the baby's diaper — his first, he'd admitted. It had been a night for firsts, she reflected. The first time Sam had kissed her.

She plunged her hands into the hot, soapy

water and began washing the dishes. A faint sound snagged her attention. Maybe Sam had finished up earlier than he'd expected. Drying her hands on a towel, she hurried into the living room and looked out the window.

Nothing.

A faint uneasiness pricked her calm. Had she heard something? Or was her imagination playing tricks on her? Thoughtfully she returned to the kitchen. In the bright fluorescent light, her fears seemed ridiculous, and she resumed washing dishes.

Without warning, the room plunged into darkness.

A chill whispered down her spine. "Get a hold of yourself," she muttered. "The lights went off. That's all. A power failure. Or the circuit breaker got flipped." She groped in a drawer for a flashlight, switched it on, and headed for the basement where the circuit breaker was located. Shining the light on it, she saw that it had been flipped. Just as she was about to switch it back on, she felt a movement at her side.

"George? Is that you?"

"It's not George, Reverend Hastings."

CHAPTER FIVE

She whirled around in the direction of the unfamiliar voice. "Who are you?"

"Someone who wants you to mind your own business." An arm clamped around her throat. "Find yourself another warehouse. Do you understand?"

She struggled to free herself, only to have the force increase. Fear had heightened her sense so that she became aware of every detail — the scratchiness of his beard against her cheek, the sickly-sweet odor of alcohol on his breath, the raspy sound of her breathing.

He wasn't big, probably no taller than she was, but he was strong, his arm a vise around her neck as she struggled to breathe. She felt herself growing faint as the flow of air into her lungs trickled into nothing. Her eyes were no longer able to focus, and she gasped for air.

"Do you understand?" the voice repeated.

She managed a nod.

The pressure at her neck eased fractionally. "Good. Now you're being smart."

"Why . . ." Her voice wouldn't work. She tried again. "Why are you doing this?"

"That's none of your business. Just remember what I told you if you want to stay healthy."

Something brushed at her legs. *George.* She gulped in air and shoved her attacker. "Get him, George."

George leaped at the intruder. The man dropped his arm, and she pushed away from him. She directed the flashlight in the direction of the fracas in time to see the assailant strike George. She lunged, trying to place herself between her dog and the attacker, but she was too late.

With a yelp of pain, George fell to the floor.

The man sprinted away, but not before he laughed harshly. "Next time it could be you, Rev."

Carla ignored him and rushed to kneel by George. She ran her hands over his head and back, her fingers encountering a large bump on the back of his head. "It's going to be all right, boy," she whispered past the lump in her throat. "It's going to be all right."

The lights switched on, and she blinked against the sudden glare.

"Carla. Carla. Where are you?"

Sam's voice. Everything was all right. Her relief was short-lived when she realized he could run into the assailant. "Watch out!"

She heard a scuffling followed by a door slamming shut.

"Carla!" Footsteps pounded down the stairs.

With the dog's head cradled in her lap, she sat stroking him, tears streaming down her face.

"Are you all right?" Sam asked.

"I'm fine," she said when he hurried to her. "It's George."

Sam picked up George and carried him upstairs. He settled the dog on the sofa and stroked his head. "You're going to be all right, boy," he said before punching out a number on the phone. After a brief conversation, he replaced the receiver and turned to Carla. "I have a friend who's a vet. He'll be here in a few minutes."

She looked at him inquiringly when he picked up the phone again.

"The police," he answered her unspoken question.

Two patrolmen arrived within a few minutes.

"You're sure you can't identify the man, Reverend Hastings?" a small, wiry officer asked.

"It was too dark."

"There was nothing in his voice, his mannerisms?" an older officer asked.

She shook her head. "I'm sorry."

"We'll have a patrol car cruise by here a couple of times tonight," the older one said, turning to Sam. "There's not much more we can do."

"Thanks."

Fifteen minutes later, the vet, John Castleton, arrived. He gently probed behind George's ears. "It's a nasty bump all right, but I don't believe it's serious." He patted the dog's head. "Just watch him for the next few hours. If he's off his food or you notice anything else unusual, give me a call. But I don't think you're going to have any problems."

"Thanks for coming by," Sam said, clapping John on the back.

"No problem. Mind telling me what's going on?"

"You'll know as soon as I do."

"Good enough." John held up a soggy piece of material. "George had this between his teeth. Didn't much want to give it up either."

114

After seeing the vet out, Sam examined the bit of blue material.

Carla eyed it. "Polyester. I can't see Barbie or Pete Hammond wearing that."

"This guy was only hired help. You can bet that the man — or woman — we want has an airtight alibi for tonight."

"You're right. What should we do now?" She didn't give him time to answer. "Give that" — she gestured to the scrap of material — "to the police. Check on each of our suspects, see whose alibi holds up, and then —"

"*We* aren't doing anything. You're going to bed. I'm going to spend some time at the computer. I've been wondering if we're approaching this from the wrong angle. We've been looking for who. Maybe we ought to try looking for why."

George woofed.

Sam scratched him behind the ears. "You saved the day."

"You hear that, George?" Carla asked, patting his side, her hand not quite steady. "You're a hero. A real hero."

George accepted the praise with a thump of his tail. He laid his head in Carla's lap before loping into the kitchen, where he picked up his towel and held it in his teeth.

He then trotted over to wait patiently by his bowl.

Sam laughed. "Okay. I guess you've earned it." He poured a generous helping of dry dog food into the dish.

With his towel anchored under his paw, George gobbled up the food. He looked up.

"No more," Sam said. "You'll get sick."

The dog walked back to Carla.

Sam lifted her in his arms and started toward the stairs. "I meant it when I said you're going to bed."

She started to protest but stopped when she felt his arms tremble around her. She realized just how frightened he'd been for her. "I'm all right, Sam. Really."

He was silent until they reached the bedroom and he set her on her feet. "I had no business leaving you alone tonight."

She heard the self-reproach in his voice. "You couldn't have known some creep was going to break in here. You can't be with me every second."

He raked his hand through his hair. "Are you sure you're okay?" Gingerly Carla touched her neck, remembering the bruising fingers that had tried to crush her.

Sam pushed her fingers aside. "Why didn't you say something about this?" he asked, his voice ominously quiet.

"It's nothing. George stopped him before . . . what are you doing?" she asked, watching as he picked up the phone.

"Calling an ambulance."

Carla took the phone from him and replaced the receiver. "Sam. Look at me." She waited until his gaze focused on her face. "I'm fine."

Gently he ran his hands over her face, touching her eyes, her lips, her cheeks. More tenderly still, he touched the sensitive area of her neck. "You're sure?"

"I'm sure."

His lips followed the path his fingers had traced, resting in the hollow of her throat. "Don't think about tonight anymore," he murmured. "The only thing that matters is that you're all right."

"If only I'd gotten a look at his face."

"I'm glad you didn't."

She looked at him with surprise, then understanding. "You think he wanted to —"

"I think tonight was a warning."

A warning.

Sam couldn't stop thinking about it as he fed information into the computer an hour later.

Next time might be the real thing. There wouldn't be a next time, he promised himself. He'd stayed with Carla until she fell asleep. For once he didn't mind George taking his customary spot at the foot of the bed. Sam had ruffled the dog's fur, silently thanking whatever fate had brought George into their lives.

Now he punched the computer keys with an urgency that was growing with every minute. He had to find the answer to why someone wanted to prevent the community home from being built. It was no longer a matter of annoying delays in buying the warehouse, now it was a matter of Carla's life.

Three hours later, he switched off the computer, more frustrated than ever. Nothing added up. Any way he looked at it, Fowler stood to come out a winner on the deal. So why was he throwing up roadblocks?

And if not him, then who?

Pete Hammond?

Sam shook his head. Much as he disagreed with Pete's politics, he still couldn't picture the senior councilman being behind the attempts to stop the community home from being built. And the attack on Carla was completely out of character for him. A man like Pete used money and power, not muscle, to get what he wanted.

Sam frowned at his reasoning. Hadn't he

told Carla that whoever had attacked her tonight was only hired help? Pete had plenty of money to buy such services. He probably had the street contacts too, which would enable him to find the right kind of help. Still, Sam couldn't fit Pete into the part.

The same arguments applied to Barbie. The woman was ambitious in her own right and undoubtedly saw her husband as her way to power. But hiring someone to threaten Carla? Barbie might wheedle and connive, but hire a thug? Sam shook his head. It didn't fit with what he knew about her. He pushed away from the desk. Having just convinced himself that none of the three suspects could be guilty, he was back at the beginning. And no closer to finding who was behind the attack on Carla.

Suddenly needing to see that she was all right, he took the steps two at a time and eased open the bedroom door. She was as he'd left her, her arm flung over her head. George looked up inquiringly from his place at the foot of the bed.

"It's all right," Sam whispered to the dog.

Apparently George understood, for he propped his head back on his paws and resumed snoring.

Seconds bled into minutes as Sam continued to stand there, unable to drag himself away. His breathing slowed as he watched her sleep, her hair spilling over the pillow in soft waves. She was safe. For now. It was his job to keep her that way. His hands clenched into fists as he thought of the animal who'd threatened her, who'd dared to put his hands on her. He'd make him pay, Sam vowed.

Quietly he closed the door behind him and started back down the stairs. He had work to do.

Tony Owens kept to the shadows, watching. So they'd called the cops. Well, he'd expected as much. He didn't mind. In fact, he was feeling pretty good. Calling the cops meant the minister and her husband were scared. If they were scared, then he'd done his job.

He grinned, thinking of the money he'd stashed inside the heating duct of his apartment. And there was more where that came from. Plenty more. All he had to do was pull a few more stunts like the one tonight and he'd be sitting pretty.

His grin died as he looked at his arm. Darn mutt had bitten right through his jacket and into the flesh. He'd better put something on it before it became infected. He'd have gotten away clean if it hadn't been for the dog.

He shook his head admiringly as he thought about the little lady minister. He had to hand it to her. She had guts. In spades. Too bad he'd had to use strong-arm tactics on her. She was a good-looking woman. If you liked the sweet-faced, innocent type.

The shadows deepened around him. The lights in the house had been extinguished, except for one on the lower level. The police had left along with some other guy. A doctor, Tony decided, judging from the small black bag he carried. Heck. He hadn't hurt the woman all that bad, just scared her.

He glanced around and decided it was time to make his exit. He lit a cigarette and started walking down the sidewalk as if he had every right to be there. None of this cloak-and-dagger stuff for him. If you wanted to hide, you did it in plain sight. That way, no one got suspicious. Sure enough, the patrol car cruised right by him. Even dared a wave to the cops inside. All he had to do was keep his cool. He'd been doing that since he was fourteen years old and on his own. He didn't even mind the sweat that trickled down his back. It kept him on his toes. A guy couldn't afford to be too laid-back.

Tony grinned suddenly. Cool and cautious. That was him.

The police dutifully bagged and labeled the scrap of blue polyester that Sam took to the precinct station the following morning.

"Can't say it'll do us much good," the duty sergeant said. "But you never know." He shrugged.

"You'll keep us informed?" Sam asked, struggling to keep hold of his temper.

"Sure. Just don't expect too much. Break-ins like this are a dime a dozen."

Sam bit back the angry words that hovered on the tip of his tongue. This was no simple break-in, he wanted to say. It was connected with the warehouse. One look at the weary lines etched on the sergeant's face told him he'd be wasting his time with explanations.

"Thanks."

The sergeant barely looked up when Sam left.

The blast of cold air that hit him as he left the precinct station did little to cool his temper as he walked the few blocks to the City Council offices. Anyone with half a brain could see this wasn't routine. Didn't they understand that Carla's life had been threatened?

His anger at the police dissolved as reason

took over. The duty sergeant was just a convenient scapegoat. Blaming the police spared Sam from acknowledging where the real blame lay — with himself. He'd vowed to protect Carla, and he'd failed. He'd put her at risk with his shortsightedness. He should have guessed that whoever was behind this would come after her. She was the force behind the community home. Without her, the movement would fizzle and die. Which was exactly what someone was counting on.

Raking his fingers through his hair, he pulled open the heavy glass doors to the City and County Building. A glance at his watch confirmed what he already knew. He was late. *Good going, Hastings,* he berated himself. He had already earned a reputation on the council as a maverick. Now he was adding to it by being late.

Sam spared a moment to stop by his office and pick up a sheaf of papers. If he was going to do battle with Pete Hammond over the community home, he wanted to be prepared.

He opened the door to the council room, hoping to slip in unnoticed.

"Nice of you to join us, Sam," Pete said with heavy sarcasm.

One of the councilwomen slid Sam a

sympathetic look and passed him a copy of the agenda.

"What's up?" Sam whispered to her.

"Your baby," she said, pointing to an item on the list. "The community home."

Sam kept his face expressionless. He'd learned early on that betraying his feelings was political suicide. Better to play his cards close to his chest. Politics, even at the city level, often involved big stakes. Not to mention even bigger egos. He smiled inwardly, thinking that he was listening to one of the biggest right now. Pete had been enormously successful in business; now he'd aimed his sights on the political arena, Sam had no quarrel with that. What he did disagree with was Pete's attempt to mix business and politics.

Pete stood, crossed to the window, and pointed in the distance. "I love this city. I think everyone here knows that. You also know that I've given a lot back to the city. I've got what you might call a vested interest in seeing that it grows. Growth is vital to a city if it's going to survive. The right kind of growth, that is."

Sam was able to interpret Pete's definition of the right kind of growth — business, industry, shopping centers. The right kind of growth did not include a home for the community's homeless. He forced his attention back to what Pete was saying.

". . . this idea for a community home is costing money. Taxpayer money."

Pete paused and looked around the room. Sam did the same thing, covertly studying the faces of the five other men and women seated around the table, trying to gauge their reaction. Two were openly bored, three others nodded in apparent agreement, another was clearly angered by Pete's words.

"Sam, maybe you'd like to give us a status report," one of the women invited.

He stood.

"Most of you know how I feel about the community home. Our city needs a place for those who have nowhere else to go. Most of these people have families with small children. Right now they're in shelters, welfare apartments, or on the streets."

One of the women shuddered.

Sam pressed home his point. "Pete, do you know what the temperature outside is right now?"

Pete looked nonplussed. "No. Should I?"

Sam turned to the rest of the council. "Anyone want to make a guess how cold it'll be tonight?" He looked at each member in turn.

Some let their gazes slide away from his;

others shook their heads.

"Try ten above zero. And that's if there's no wind chill factor. If there is, make it ten below. Maybe twenty."

He let the impact of his words sink in.

"The community home is a beginning. A small one, but a beginning all the same. It isn't about dollars and cents. It's about people. And how we feel about them. Most of all, it represents hope. Hope for people who don't have much else. Can we deny them that?"

He heard murmurs of approval mixed with an angry buzz of disagreement.

"Sam, maybe you'd answer a question for me," Pete said.

Sam leaned against the corner of the table. "Sure."

"Who's really behind this idea for a community home? You?" Pete paused significantly. "Or your wife?"

Sam took his time. He knew the others were waiting to see how he fielded Pete's question. He also knew there was more riding on this than the community home. His position on the City Council was at stake.

"We both are, Pete, because we both care about the people in this city. Let me ask you a question."

"Shoot."

"Why are you so against it?"

Pete sat back in his chair, arms folded across his chest. He didn't bother answering the question. He merely glared at Sam.

"Thank you, Sam," the chairman said. "You've given us a lot to think about." He glanced at the agenda. "Let's move on now to the next item."

The next hour was spent discussing whether to raise the police chief's salary and buy an additional fire truck. The council was split down the middle on both issues. When someone moved to adjourn the meeting, it was quickly seconded.

"Good job," one of the councilwomen whispered to Sam on her way out as he gathered up his papers.

"Thanks."

Acting on an impulse, Sam stopped by Horace Fowler's office on the way home.

"Sam Hastings to see Mr. Fowler."

A gray-haired, grandmotherly secretary greeted him. "I'm sorry, Mr. Hastings. Mr. Fowler is out now. Could I help you? I'm Sarah Barclay, Mr. Fowler's personal secretary."

Sam stabbed his fingers through his hair and loosened the scarf around his neck.

"No . . . thanks. I'll try again another time."

"Would you like a cup of coffee?"

He had two more stops to make, but the offer of coffee sounded too good to pass up. "Thanks." He shrugged off his damp overcoat, hanging it and his scarf on the coat tree.

Sarah bustled around, pouring him a cup of coffee, inquiring about sugar and cream.

Sam smiled, remembering Carla's description of her: *a plump little sparrow.* It fit.

"My wife mentioned how helpful you were when she was here."

Sarah beamed. "How nice of her. She's a lovely woman. So kind and compassionate."

Sam nodded, his interest focused on the pictures hanging on the walls that depicted various buildings around the city. He recognized a new condominium complex, a downtown skyrise, the plans for an outlet mall — all multimillion-dollar investments. Fowler had his finger in a lot of pies. So why was he holding onto an abandoned warehouse?

Sarah must have sensed his curiosity, for she nodded toward one of the bigger pictures. "That's our newest acquisition. The Bayside Complex."

"Mr. Fowler appears to have done very

well for himself."

For a moment, he thought he saw a shadow pass over Sarah's face before she smiled again. "Yes, he has. He's very . . . astute."

Sam drained the rest of his coffee and set down the cup. "I'd better be going. Thanks again for the coffee."

"You're most welcome. Please give Reverend Hastings my regards." She handed him his coat and scarf. "What a beautiful scarf. It looks handmade."

"It is." He smiled. "A present from my wife."

He was still smiling as he left Fowler's office. His visit had netted him a big fat zero, but he wasn't thinking about Fowler now. He was thinking about Carla. His lips hardened into a tight line. No one was going to hurt her.

With that thought in mind, he detoured to the shelter. There was a chance, a slim one, he admitted, he might learn something more. He scanned the dining room for the man who'd issued the warning last week. When he failed to find him, he went in search of Jared.

He ran into Hank Walker instead.

"Hastings, I'm glad you're here. I need to talk with you." Hank steered Sam to a corner where they'd have relative privacy. "I. . . uh . . . I appreciate you getting me that job at the warehouse. But I won't be coming back."

"What's wrong?"

Walker looked over his shoulder, obviously uneasy. "They said they'd come after Lorna, Jared's ma. And then Jared."

"Who's they?"

"I don't know. I just found a note in my lunch bucket." He gripped Sam's arm. "I ain't scared for myself. I grew up around the docks. There's not much I ain't seen or done. I've been taking care of myself ever since I can remember. But Lorna and Jared . . ."

"Hank, you don't have to explain —"

"I'm no coward. But when it comes to my wife and my boy, I can't take no chances." Hank let his shoulders slump.

Sam's heart went out to the man. He couldn't fault him for wanting to protect his family. "I don't blame you, Hank. Let me see what I can do. There may be something at a construction project a friend of mine is in charge of."

A dull color crept up the man's cheeks. "I couldn't ask you to do that. Not after I let you down."

"You didn't let me down. You did what

you had to do to protect your family. No one can ask for more than that."

"Thanks. You're all right, Hastings."

Sam broke every speed limit on his way home. Once there, he strode into the kitchen.

Carla looked up from where she was stirring something at the stove.

"I'm glad —"

He took her in his arms and crushed her to him.

"Sam? Sam, what's wrong?"

"You're all right."

"Of course I'm all right. Why wouldn't I be?"

Her hands and cheeks were cold. "Where were you?"

"Marianne Lindquist called. She needed someone to stay with Emilie while she went to the store."

"And you went, even after what's happened?" He tightened his hold on her.

"Sam, you're scaring me."

"Don't you get it? I *want* you to be scared. I want you to be so scared you'll stay out of it." His voice softened. "*I'm* scared you're going to be the next victim. If anything happened to you . . ."

When she pulled away, he looked at her quizzically.

"I love you, Sam. You know that. But I can't stop being what I am. I have a duty to the members of my congregation. They depend on me. If I cringed in a corner every time I was scared, I wouldn't be able to function." She touched the collar that hugged her neck. "This is what I am. This is who I am."

He heard the next words as loudly as if she'd said them aloud. *You knew that when you married me.*

He saw in her eyes that she knew he understood. But understanding her commitment to her job and accepting that it could put her in danger were miles apart.

"I love what you are, who you are. That's why . . ." His voice broke. He cleared his throat and tried again. "That's why I can't let anything happen to you."

She cradled his head against her shoulder.

CHAPTER SIX

"I forgot my notes for my sermon."

Sam swung his truck into the church parking lot on Friday night. "I'll get them for you."

"You'd never find them on my desk," Carla said. "I meant to clean it out today, but —"

"You were called to the hospital. When are you ever going to learn to say no?"

She smiled. "When you do."

"I don't —" He smiled sheepishly. "Okay. You got me."

"Good."

Sam opened her door and helped her out of the truck. "Jared's mom needed a ride to the doctor and I took her. No big deal." He took her arm to help her over the slippery patches of ice that pockmarked the asphalt.

"And Mrs. Miller just had surgery. She needed someone to be there for her. No big deal," she mimicked his words.

"Did anyone ever tell you that you're impossible to argue with?"

"Only you." She fumbled in her purse for the key to the church. Turning it in the lock, she pushed open the door. She had flipped on the light switches and started toward the front of the chapel when she saw it.

Scarlet and black letters scarred the walls. Crude pictures punctuated the words. It took her a moment before she realized what she was seeing. And the significance of it. Bile rose in her throat at the viciousness of the words. Never before had she been the target of such hatred.

She read the mildest of the warnings: *Preachers belong in church, not in warehouses.* Other threats were more explicit, describing in detail what would happen to her if she didn't let go of the idea of turning the warehouse into a community home. The vileness of the words caused her to blanch.

Sam took her arm. "Carla, let me take you home. You can't do anything now."

She shook off his hand. She couldn't hide from this; the filth surrounded her, invading the place most sacred to her. She had to know what she was dealing with. She'd always believed that understanding one's enemy was the first step in forgiving him. But she couldn't understand this enemy, no matter how hard she tried. She wandered from the chapel into the vestry, ending her tour in the Sunday school room.

Sam accompanied her. He didn't say a word. Only the lines bracketing his mouth betrayed his anger.

Intellectually she understood that greed was the motive behind the vandalism. But her heart had a much harder time accepting it. How could anyone want a piece of property so much as to be willing to desecrate a church? She went back to the chapel, where the damage seemed to be concentrated. Unwillingly she lifted her gaze to the pulpit. The ugly words jumped out at her.

Mind your own business or else.

The graffiti was crude. It also showed talent. Carla tried to focus on that, rather than the vulgar messages. The wasted talent caused her as much pain as the obscenities sprayed on the walls. She couldn't help the tears that gathered in the corners of her eyes. She swiped at them with the back of her hand, but not before some had spilled down her cheeks.

Tenderly Sam kissed them away. "It'll be all right. We'll paint over it."

She looked at the bold red images outlined in black and shook her head. "Nothing's going to cover that."

"We'll find a way." He folded her into his arms.

She rested there, drawing on his strength. She felt her own slipping away and was powerless to stop it. First the warehouse fire. And now this. For the first time she wondered if she could be wrong in her commitment to helping the city's homeless. If her stubbornness resulted in this kind of vandalism to the church, did she have the right to continue? What about all the members of the congregation who attended church faithfully every Sunday? They deserved a place to worship, a sanctuary from the outside world.

She remembered the Saturday when people from all over the community joined together to paint the church. Slowly the cracked, peeling surface had been covered with sparkling white paint. Young and old alike had wielded brushes. The more skilled had painted the trim and eaves a dark blue. The workers had moved inside, giving the dark rooms a fresh coat of paint. The result was something the whole community had been proud of, members and nonmembers alike.

"What kind of monster does something

like this?" she asked, her voice a thread of sound.

"Someone who's running scared."

Sam's words surprised her. She hadn't thought of it that way. He was right. With that realization, she knew she couldn't give in to whomever was behind this.

She raised her gaze once more to look at the crude artwork and its sinister message. The bold colors seemed to mesmerize her, and she blinked to wipe their impact from her mind.

Sam took her hand. "Come on. I'm taking you home."

She tugged it away. "I can't go home. Someone's got to start cleaning this up."

"Someone will. But it's not going to be you. Not today. You've had about as much as you can take."

Unwillingly she admitted he was right. Tomorrow, she promised herself. Tomorrow she'd start the fight again. Her hand found Sam's. "Let's go home."

Sam insisted on making dinner while she soaked in a bath. There she could almost imagine that the vandalism was only a bad dream. Almost.

The bathwater turned tepid, but she didn't stir. She needed the peace, the solitude. There would be time enough later to face what needed to be done. A chill shivered down her spine, but she didn't fool herself into believing that its source was the rapidly cooling water. Never before had she been the object of such hatred. It was more than the implied threat of violence, though, that had her trembling. It was the desecration of something holy, something that should have commanded the respect of even the most hardened heart.

Because of her, that profanity had been targeted at the church. Her earlier resolve quavered as she questioned her motives. Had she pushed for the community home because she genuinely wanted to help others, or was it for a more personal reason — a selfish desire to have her name connected with such an accomplishment? A week ago, even a day ago, she would never have asked herself this question. She had been certain of what she was doing and why. Such confidence now seemed naive, even arrogant. If she didn't feel so much like crying, she'd laugh at herself.

She put the question to herself. It seemed imperative that she find the answer. Slowly she shook her head. Right now, she wasn't sure. She wasn't even sure she *wanted* to know the answer. She wasn't given a chance to ponder the question any longer, because

Sam called to her from outside the door.

Over soup and sandwiches, they talked of everything but the vandalism, skirting it with a finesse Carla didn't know she possessed. Sam must have understood how she felt, for he respected her unspoken wish and didn't bring up the subject. She pushed her food around on the plate, aware that she wasn't fooling him but feeling she had to make the effort. He deserved that much. When she knew she couldn't pretend any longer, she looked up at him. What she felt must have shown on her face, for he took her hand and led her upstairs. There she curled up in bed.

She thought he intended to leave her to her grief, but he stayed. Settling himself against the headboard, he pulled her into the shelter of his arms. He talked, rambling about things that had happened at work, the news from the City Council, the latest about Jared and his family. She listened to the flow of small talk, knowing what he was doing, and she was grateful for it.

Almost imperceptibly she felt the tension begin to seep from her. She closed her eyes, letting the soft stream of words swirl around her. His voice washed over her. The gentle cadence of words continued, an invitation to forget the pain and ugliness of the last hours.

She gave in to the temptation of sleep. In the oblivion of sleep, there'd be no hateful messages scrawled across the walls of the church. There'd be no selfish interests trying to block the building of the community home. There'd be no pain or evil. There'd be only peace.

She was wrong.

Her dreams were slashes of red and black, the monstrous words scratched across the church walls come to life. She tried to fight her way clear of the demons.

They were her enemy. But they closed in on her, clawing, scraping, yanking at her until she felt herself pulled into a sea churning with waves of red tipped with black. She flailed her arms against the drag of the current, but she was powerless to save herself. She was drowning. Drowning in a sea of blood. She gasped for breath when, without warning, the scene switched. And the enemy changed.

She saw herself.

Bloody words dripped from a mirror where she looked at her reflection, her face contorted into a grotesque mask. Instinctively she knew she didn't want to see the words, but she forced herself to read them.

She wasn't surprised to find them all the same.

Pride.

Pride.

Pride.

She turned away from the view, but she was surrounded by mirrors, the words following her, mocking her.

"No!"

Strong hands gripped her shoulders. "Carla. Carla, wake up. It's Sam."

Caught in the web of the nightmare, she fought him, but he only held her more tightly until, at last, she sagged against him.

"Sam?"

"It's all right, sweetheart." He stroked her hair, pushing it away from her face.

She was hot and sticky, her nightgown plastered to her, her hair damp.

"I'll be right back," he said and disappeared into the bathroom. When he returned, he patted her face with a cool cloth. "Better?"

She managed a small nod.

"Want to tell me about it?"

"No." She thought about the dream. And what it said about her. "Yes."

"Which is it?"

"I dreamed about the words."

"Don't think about them."

"Not those words."

"Which ones?"

Moonlight spilled into the room, turning his face into a study of light and shadow. She saw the puzzlement in his eyes. How did she explain to him what she barely understood herself?

"Which words?" he asked again.

"Pride. Mine." Slowly, haltingly, the self-doubts came out. "Don't you see? I'm to blame for what happened at the church. If I hadn't been so set on having the community home built, none of this would have happened."

"You don't know that."

She shook off his hands. "I know. I know it was my pride that caused it."

"Wanting to build a decent place for people to live isn't pride, Carla. It's humanity. It's what makes you what you are."

She thought about that. Was Sam right? Or was he only trying to spare her more pain? She raised her gaze to his. What she found in his eyes was truth. And love.

Against Sam's wishes, she walked to the church the following day. He insisted on accompanying her. The cold, crisp air and pristine white of newly fallen snow tempted her to believe that last night was a nightmare, one that would disappear in the day-light.

But the sun shone on the church with merciless brightness, and they saw what hadn't been visible last night. Lurid green and purple images covered the exterior of the church, a stark contrast to the white walls.

She bit back a gasp.

Sam muttered something under his breath.

"How could anyone be so sick?" she asked, nearly choking on the words as she looked at the hideous figures and profanities defacing the walls.

Slowly she circled the church. Each side had received the same hideous treatment.

"We can't do anything today," Sam said. "We need help."

She nodded, knowing he was right. The obscenities silently shouted at her, mocking everything she believed in. It would take more than the two of them to cover the ugliness that confronted them. But it was the ugliness inside her that caused her greater pain. Could she stand in front of the congregation tomorrow and preach words of love when her heart was filled with anger? And, if she did, what did that make her? The

Bible was scathing in its condemnation of hypocrites.

For a moment, she considered feigning sickness tomorrow. The services would be canceled, and she'd have another week before she had to face the people who looked to her for spiritual leadership.

Coward.

Hypocrite or coward? She wanted to laugh but was afraid it would turn into a sob. Prayer had always provided answers in the past, but now she shunned the idea of kneeling and asking for help.

On Sunday, Carla slipped her clerical robe over her dress, automatically straightening the pleats and adjusting the collar. Her reflection in the mirror did little to reassure her. Her face was pale, her eyes dark and haunted-looking, her lips trembling. As she entered the chapel, she quickly took her place, unable to shake hands or greet people as was her custom. The choir opened the service with a hymn, their normally exuberant voices oddly subdued. Carla clasped her hands, silently praying for strength.

Could she face these people whom she'd promised to serve, knowing she was the cause of the violence that greeted them? She heard the whispers, the mumblings, the occasional sob. She also heard anger. It was the anger that resonated within her. She identified with it all too well. Understanding that it was her enemy, she tamped it down. Anger and hate were behind the vandalism. They would not defeat it; only love could do that. She, who'd spent her adult life preaching forgiveness, now wondered if she had simply mouthed empty words, unable to practice what she claimed to believe.

She began, and her voice quavered, just as she'd feared. She'd never be heard over the murmurings from the congregation. She felt the color creep into her cheeks. The text blurred before her eyes. She looked at the sea of faces, trying to focus on one at a time. There were Maude and Ethan, their eyes full of compassion. Sitting next to them were Mrs. Miller and the rest of the blue-haired ladies who were the backbone of the church committees. Carla saw a smile, a thumbs-up gesture, a slight nod of the head. She felt the energy build within her at these small signs of support. They didn't blame her.

She swallowed and started again. Her voice gathered strength as she read from the Bible. She didn't need it; the passage she'd chosen from the Gospel of Saint Matthew was one she'd memorized long ago. Finally she closed the leather-bound book. She stepped away from the pulpit, needing to close the distance between herself and the congregation.

"It's easy to preach forgiveness. Putting it into practice is much harder."

An amen from somewhere in the congregation punctuated her words.

"For the past two days I've lived with anger in my heart. This morning, that anger was still there. It burned so brightly that I doubted my ability to stand before you. The anger is gone now. But it didn't disappear magically." She paused. "You banished it."

She heard the small gasps that rippled through the chapel. "You banished it with your understanding, your support, your faith in me. I came here ready to offer my resignation as pastor. I believed I had cost you your church." A murmur of protest spread through the congregation. She swallowed around the lump in her throat. "What I saw in your eyes — and your hearts — convinced me that I was wrong."

"Amen, Reverend." Ethan's deep voice carried over the quieter expressions of approval.

She turned to smile in his direction. "Thank you, Ethan. Thank you all for your support and belief in me." For a moment, she let her gaze settle on Sam, who stood quietly at the rear of the church. The love and pride she saw in his eyes caused her to catch her breath.

"I wish that love and forgiveness were enough to undo the damage that's been done. But faith alone won't rid our church of the filth that covers our walls. This coming Saturday, we're having a work party. Anyone who wants to help is invited." No longer able to hold back her tears, she felt them stream down her face.

When she looked up, she discovered she wasn't the only one who was crying. Soft sobs mingled with amens. She didn't wipe away her tears. They were a testament to the love she felt from these people, a tangible sign that good could triumph over evil. The choir closed with a hymn. Carla tried to sing and found she couldn't. Her throat was thick with emotion. She found her voice long enough to offer the benediction. Following the prayer, she walked down the center aisle, pausing as people reached out to press her hand. Gnarled hands of the elderly; small, soft hands of children; callused hands of people who knew hard work intimately, all found their way to hers.

She stood at the door, thanking all those who had come, accepting their words of love, comfort, and support.

"Don't you worry," said Mr. Porter, the church custodian. "We'll get this mess cleaned up. Make the church look better than ever." He shuffled, a clear sign he wanted to say more. "I don't mind telling you, Reverend, I was plenty mad this morning. Guess I still am. But you made me see it for what it was. I thank you for it."

Carla looked at this gruff man, who normally used as few words as possible, and felt fresh tears prick her eyes.

"We'll come through this," Mrs. Miller said, kissing Carla on the cheek. "I'll be here Saturday. I can still paint with the best of them."

Carla clung to the older woman briefly. Mrs. Miller was the worst gossip in the church, but she also had one of the biggest hearts.

Maude and Ethan were among the last to leave. Maude squeezed Carla's hand. "Let yourself grieve, honey. You've got a right. Then get out there and do what you do best. Fight for what you believe in."

"We'll be here on Saturday," Ethan said and hugged her awkwardly. "You know, you're like the daughter we never had. Maude and I . . . Well, you just let us know how we can help."

"Thank you," Carla whispered.

Sam watched her, so proud that he felt he would burst. He wanted to take her in his arms and twirl her around and around, but he kept to the background, understanding that Carla needed this time with the people she served so selflessly. She'd been prepared to accept the censure of the members of her congregation, even to tender her resignation. Now she deserved to welcome their love.

"You were magnificent," he said when they were finally alone.

She shook her head. "It wasn't me. It was the people. They made it happen. Without them, I'd still be wasting my energy on anger." She touched his cheek. "Without you, I wouldn't have had the courage to be here."

He wasn't surprised at the way she attributed the morning's success to others. That was Carla's way. She was incapable of claiming a victory for herself. It was one of the reasons he loved her as he did.

That very love for others that was so much a part of her had caused him more than one sleepless night. Despite the threats made against her, she still didn't fully accept the possibility that someone wanted to harm her. She'd been devastated over the damage to the church, but she'd passed over the warnings directed at her with scarcely a thought.

She'd insisted on keeping to her regular schedule of visiting homebound church members, volunteering at the hospital, and serving meals at the shelter. So far there'd been no more incidents. But he wasn't about to discount the warnings. Someone wanted to stop the work at the warehouse. That same someone saw Carla as a threat. They'd have to come through him to get to her, Sam vowed.

CHAPTER SEVEN

Saturday morning was bright with energy and enthusiasm. Workers armed with scrub brushes, solvent, and paint descended on the church. After much discussion, they'd decided to tackle the exterior first.

Dressed in her oldest jeans and one of Sam's flannel shirts, Carla perched on top of a ladder, trying to stretch far enough to reach the tip of one of the more lurid pictures with her brush.

Mr. Porter steadied the ladder for her from the ground. "Reverend Hastings, you got no business being up there. If the mister was to see you, he'd have my hide. Yours too."

"I'm perfectly all right," she called down. "Just another minute and I'll be finished."

She suppressed a guilty twinge as she acknowledged the truth of Mr. Porter's words. Sam *would* have a fit if he knew she were perched on a rickety ladder two stories above the ground. No one else had volunteered for the job, so she'd scrambled up the ladder, doing her best to ignore the queasy feeling in her stomach whenever she looked down. Sam had gone to pick up Jared and would be back any minute. With that thought in mind, she hurried to finish the last bit.

She dipped her brush in the gallon can of paint, which she had balanced on the top rung. One more swipe and she'd be done. She drew the brush over the offensive picture and its equally obnoxious message, determined that none of the vicious words would remain. Seeing the sparkling white paint eat up the green and purple images gave her a feeling of immense satisfaction.

"Done."

"Easy does it," Mr. Porter called. "Just back on down."

"Piece of cake," she shouted back. At that moment, her foot caught on the ladder rung, tipping over the gallon of paint.

"Look out," she yelled.

The can of paint plunged to the ground. She spared a moment to see if Mr. Porter had managed to move out of the way fast enough. What she saw caused her heart to jump up to her throat.

"Oh, no."

"Oh, yes," an irate voice called up to her.

Sam. A very mad Sam, glossy white paint dripping down his hair, his face, his clothes.

She hurried down the ladder.

"What are you doing up there?" Large hands caught her around the waist and swung her down the few remaining feet.

She decided to ignore that. "Are you all right?"

"I'm great. I always wear a gallon of paint."

"I'm sorry. My foot got caught and . . ." She couldn't help it. A laugh bubbled up inside her. She sucked in her cheeks in an attempt to contain it, but it erupted in a gust of merriment.

Sam glared at her.

She grabbed the rag she'd tucked in her jeans pocket and started to dab at his face.

"Reverend Hastings . . . I mean, Carla . . . I don't want to tell you what to do or nothing, but I think maybe you're making things worse," Jared said, a grin spreading over his face.

She looked at her handiwork, chagrined to find that he was right. She'd succeeded in spreading the paint rather than removing it.

By now the rest of the workers had gathered around them. A few snickers could be heard. Eyes downcast, Carla tried to look properly repentant. Judging from Sam's expression, she decided she wasn't very successful.

"I am sorry," she said once more.

He gave a rueful smile. "I think I've been christened. Again." His gaze sought hers, reminding her of the evening when he'd helped her baby-sit the Lindquists' baby. While he'd been holding her, little Emilie Lindquist had wet her diaper, right through to Sam's shirt.

Heedless of the paint that covered him, Carla wrapped her arms around him. "I love you."

"Me too."

He kissed her soundly on the lips.

A cheer from the onlookers made them break apart. She didn't feel self-conscious about the kiss, as she once would have. Now she felt only a deep sense of satisfaction. And love. Always that.

"Hey, Reverend, I hate to break this up, but we've got a church to paint." Mr. Porter was grinning from ear to ear.

She grinned back. "You're right. As soon as Sam and I get cleaned up a bit —"

"We can do it right here." Sam picked up a hose and turned it on himself, washing off the worst of the paint, before aiming it at her.

She tried to fend off the spray of water before giving up and letting the water wash over her. "Guess I deserved that," she said, wiping her eyes. Someone handed her a towel, and she dried her face and hair. "Okay. Let's get our church painted."

They ended up changing their clothes, their wet, paint-splattered clothes catching and holding the sharp breeze that whipped through the city.

Two hours later, Carla checked her watch, frowning when she remembered that she hadn't taken time to walk George that morning. She'd let him out for only a few minutes.

"Jared, would you mind walking George? He's probably lonely all by himself." She pulled her keys from her pocket and handed them to the boy.

"You bet," he said, racing off.

Ethan and Maude showed up around noon, bearing dozens of Maude's home-made doughnuts.

After they'd been distributed to everyone, Carla bit into one appreciatively. The still-warm pastry melted in her mouth. "I think I've died and gone to heaven." She sighed dramatically.

Maude flushed with pleasure. "We thought you might need a snack."

"You thought right," Sam said, downing his own in two bites.

Jared returned with George, who danced about with his usual exuberance. He jumped up on Ethan, his paws landing on the elderly man's chest, pushing him down.

Sam helped him up. "You all right, Ethan?"

"Dern dog knocked me on my —"

"Ethan!"

Sam and Carla traded smiles at the warning in Maude's voice.

Ethan snorted. "On the other side of my lap," he finished with a harumph, rubbing the injured area.

"You're sure you're all right?" Carla asked.

He snorted again. "Take more than that to get rid of me. We're here to help, and help we're going to do."

"I'm sorry about George. Sometimes he gets a little excited." She ignored Sam's grunt and turned to the culprit. "George, what are we going to do with you?"

He gave her a pitiful look and eyed the plate of doughnuts with such longing that she couldn't refuse. "One doughnut, and then you go home. Understand?"

He woofed.

Maude, Carla, Sam, and Jared all laughed at the haste with which George scarfed down the doughnut.

"It's not George's fault. He just wanted a doughnut," Jared said, munching on one. "No one cooks like Grandma Maude." He clapped a hand to his mouth. "I mean, you cook real good too, Carla. It's just that —"

"It's all right, Jared. You're right. No one cooks like Maude."

Maude beamed and passed around a second helping of doughnuts to everyone.

Ethan chuckled. "Guess I can't blame a dog for doing what comes naturally." He reached for another doughnut, but Maude slapped his hand away.

"You've had enough, old man. You know what the doctor said about your cholesterol."

He harumphed again. "Dang doctors want to take all the fun out of everything."

With an effort, Carla kept a straight face. She chanced a look at Sam, discovering he too was struggling with a smile.

"Okay, George, it's home for you," Sam said.

George barked plaintively.

Carla steeled herself to ignore the hurt expression in his eyes. Although he'd made a lot of progress in the weeks they'd had him, he still cried whenever he felt left out. She didn't buy Sam's theory that George was a master manipulator. He was just an oversize baby who needed a lot of love and attention to make up for his earlier neglect.

Jared took George home, looking glum when he returned a few minutes later. "George didn't like missing out on all the fun. I had to promise him an extra lap around the park tomorrow."

"I think he'll survive," Sam said dryly.

What the workers lacked in expertise they made up for in eagerness. Under strict instructions from Sam that she was not to climb any more ladders, Carla gave up her place to Jared, who clambered up the ladder with the dexterity of a monkey shimmying up a tree. She grinned at his eagerness to show off his skills.

Her smile faded as she saw the lines of fatigue on Maude and Ethan's faces. They'd been working tirelessly for the last three hours, washing out brushes, moving drop cloths, doing everything but the actual painting. She knew they needed to rest, but how could she suggest it without hurting their feelings? She saw Sam watching them, a slight frown on his face.

"Ethan, I wonder if you and Maude would mind running down to the pizza parlor and

ordering enough pizza and pop for everyone?" he asked, pulling some bills out of his
wallet. "I thought we'd probably better
order early to get enough for this crowd. I'd
do it, but the boss" — he winked in Carla's
direction — "would get mad at me if I left
my post."

"Sure thing," Ethan said. "Anything else
you need?"

Sam shook his head. "That's all, thanks.
Can you bring them back around six?"

Ethan pocketed the money. "You got it."

Carla watched the exchange silently. After
thanking them for coming and seeing them
off, she gave Sam a hug.

"What's that for?"

"For being you." She picked up her paintbrush and made a face. "Back to work."

"You're a hard woman, Carla Hastings."

She wielded the paintbrush like a weapon.
"You'd better believe it."

Three hours later, the last bit of graffiti
had been obliterated. She laid down her
brush and stretched out the kinks in her
arms and shoulders. Pushing back her hair,
she started to rub the back of her neck
where the pain was centered. Strong hands
gently pushed hers aside, kneading the
tender area between her shoulder blades.
She reached for Sam's hand, holding it for

159

a moment. He squeezed hers before resuming the massage.

She sighed in pleasure. "Thanks."

"It looks great. Everyone did a good job," he said.

"It's more than that. It's a miracle." They looked at the freshly painted church. It gleamed in the soft light of the waning sun. "This could have torn our church apart. Instead everyone pulled together."

"*You* got them to do that."

"It's the people. They're pretty special."

"They are at that," he agreed. "Come on. Let's get cleaned up. I'm starved."

After washing out the brushes and folding up the tarps, they joined the others in the church's recreation hall, where people sat picnic-style on the floor.

"What about the inside of the church, Reverend?" one of the church elders asked. "What are we going to do about that? It's a mess, what with all those disgusting words and dirty pictures."

Some of her earlier satisfaction faded as she acknowledged his point. The outside of the church was finished, but the interior still awaited them. The vandals had intensified the viciousness of their work as they'd moved inside.

"We'll do just what we did today. Work

together." She knew it was a lame answer, but it was the best she had.

"That's right," Ethan said. Looking rested, he and Maude had returned with the pizza and sodas. "As long as we stick together, we can do anything." He wagged a piece of pepperoni pizza in the other man's face. "You just wait and see."

Carla smiled at him gratefully. She could always depend on Ethan and Maude to back her up. By eight o'clock, everyone but Carla, Sam, and Jared had gone home. Quietly they cleaned up the pizza leftovers and trash.

While Carla went to her office to add a few last-minute notes to tomorrow's sermon, Sam took a last look through the church. He examined the obscene pictures that filled the chapel's interior. The graffiti marring the outside of the church had been hastily and poorly applied, probably due to the frigid temperatures that had blanketed the city that night. Painting over it had been fairly easy. By contrast, the pictures defacing the church's interior had been carefully stroked, layer upon layer, until they seemed to leap right off the walls. The vandals had been lavish with their use of paint.

Jared joined him, his hair stiff with daubs

of paint. "White paint's not going to cover it."

Jared's observation coincided with Sam's own. Painting over the graffiti might subdue the profane messages, but it wouldn't erase them. "Got any suggestions?"

Jared appeared to study it. "How 'bout we paint a mural over it? You know — scenes from the Bible. Noah's ark. Moses and the Ten Commandments. There's a bunch of neat stories in the Bible that would make great pictures. Maybe do a history from the time of Adam on." He laughed shortly. "We could probably cover the Old Testament and New Testament with all these walls to do."

Sam looked at the boy with increased respect. "I think you've got something there."

Jared squared his shoulders and held his head a little higher. "You really think so?"

"You bet I do." Sam dropped a hand on the boy's shoulder. "Tell me something. How come you know so much about the Bible?"

"My mom took me to Sunday school every week when I was little. Guess some of that stuff stuck with me."

"I'm glad some of that stuff stuck with him," Carla said as Sam relayed the conversation to her after he'd taken Jared home.

"Yeah."

"Now we've got just one problem left."

"What's that?"

"Where are we going to find someone who can do the murals? We can't afford a professional artist. After all we spent on paint, we can't afford anyone."

Sam grinned. He'd saved the best for last. "What if I told you he's going to start Monday?"

"Monday?"

"That's what I said." He smiled smugly.

"Who is it?"

He continued smiling, only shaking his head when she pressed him.

She pretended to twist his arm behind his back. "Had enough?" she asked in a tough-guy voice.

"Okay." He gave an exaggerated wince. "You got it out of me."

Hands on hips, she waited.

"It's Jared."

"Jared paints?"

"He's a regular Michelangelo."

She looked skeptical.

"Well, maybe he has a little ways to go before that, but the kid's got real talent. He showed me some of his work tonight when I took him home."

"You're a genius."

"Well, maybe part genius."

"And modest too." She poked him lightly on the arm.

"To a fault."

"Last week, I didn't know what we were going to do. Now it's all coming together." She spread her arms open.

Sam took her hand. "Come on. You've been on your feet for fourteen hours."

"So have you."

"I have bigger feet."

"What kind of logic is that?"

"My kind." He skimmed his knuckles over her cheek. "How do you do it?"

"Do what?"

"Manage to look so beautiful after you've spent the day painting." She wore no makeup, her hair was pulled back with a ribbon, and she was the most beautiful woman he'd ever seen.

"You're full of blarney. You're also trying to change the subject."

"Guilty as charged. Now will you go to bed before you drop, or do I have to carry you?"

"Are you coming?" she asked.

"I've got some work to do." He dropped a kiss on her cheek. "Don't wait up."

He spent the next several hours catching up on all the work he'd postponed during the last week. He leaned back in his chair, fingers steepled over his chest. The day had been successful, but it didn't bring them any closer to figuring out who was behind the threats. Protecting Carla had become a full-time job, one made more difficult because he couldn't let her know he was doing it. He knew the reaction *that* would receive. She'd deny the need for protection, tell him that she could take care of herself, and go about business as usual.

So far, she'd accepted his explanation that he'd decided to take a few days off work so he could spend more time with Jared. She'd been so preoccupied with worrying about the church, she hadn't seen through his subterfuge. But she'd grow suspicious if he kept up the pretense much longer.

"What's all this?" Carla asked the next morning.

Sam looked at the newly installed modem and fax machine. "I . . . uh . . . decided to start working at home more. Hope you don't mind my bringing all this stuff in."

"Of course not. I'm just surprised. That's all."

"It means I'll have that much more time to spend with my favorite preacher lady."

"Well, the preacher lady thanks you," she

said quietly. "She also knows what you're up to."

Sam assumed his best innocent look. "And what would that be?"

"Making sure I'm not alone." All the banter had vanished from her voice.

"You knew all the time, didn't you?"

She nodded. "I love you for it."

"You don't mind?"

"How could I mind? You're only trying to keep me safe."

Sam didn't bother to hide his sigh of relief. "Just think of it as a reason for us to spend more time together."

"Only a fool would argue with that."

The following day, Carla pulled on her coat, preparing to go to the church.

"Where are you going?" Sam asked, looking up from the computer monitor.

"The church. I want to see how Jared's doing."

"Uh-uh. It's off-limits until he's all done."

"Sam, I'm the minister. I have to go to the church."

"Not this week, you don't."

She planted her hands on her hips. "What about my counseling? The Bible study group? The —"

"They'll meet here."

When Sam proved he had an answer for all of her objections, she finally gave up. "If I die of suspense, it'll be on your head," she said darkly.

"I'll take the risk."

On Saturday morning, Sam gave her the go-ahead.

Carla insisted they call Jared before going to the church. He deserved to be there. When Sam left to pick Jared up, she cautioned herself not to expect too much. After all, Jared was only a teenage boy with no formal training in art. As long as he'd covered the awful pictures, it didn't really matter what he painted over them. She wasn't prepared for what she saw when she stepped inside.

"It's beautiful, Jared," Carla said around the lump in her throat. "How did you do it in such a short time?"

Jared blushed. "It wasn't that h-hard," he stammered. "Sam bought all the paints and brushes. All I had to do was paint the pictures."

Sam looped an arm around Jared's shoulders. "You did a lot more than just paint pictures."

The mural depicted a history of the Bible. All the stories were there, painted in loving detail: Adam and Eve's expulsion from the Garden of Eden, the great flood, Jonah in the belly of the whale, Moses parting the Red Sea, and more.

Carla followed the progression through the chapel, into the Sunday school room, finally ending in the vestry. No trace of the vandalism remained.

She turned and hugged Jared. "Thank you. You've given us back our church."

Jared's blush deepened. "I enjoyed it."

"I can't wait for everyone to see it on Sunday," she said. "Do you think you and your parents can come?"

Jared looked at Sam. "I . . . uh . . . if you think it's all right, sure."

"Of course it's all right."

"Come on, we'd better get you home," Sam said. "Seems like I remember you have a big history final to study for."

Jared groaned.

Carla kept the news of the murals to herself until Sunday morning. The congregation hummed with excitement as she stood to give her sermon. At the conclusion, she asked Jared to join her.

"This is the young man we have to thank for the beautiful murals. I hope you'll each take the opportunity to thank him."

The choir finished with a hymn.

Carla took her customary place at the door, with one difference: Jared was at her side, obviously embarrassed but pleased by all the praise heaped on him.

"They're painting the church." The boss's voice snapped with anger.

Tony took a deep breath. "What did you expect? That they'd leave it that way? Those kids I hired trashed it but good."

"I expected you to make sure the good reverend and her husband gave up."

"The lady's a fighter." Tony couldn't quite keep the respect from his voice, though he knew the boss wouldn't like it. Still, he had to hand it to the lady. She didn't back down easy. He admired that. Even if it did make his job harder. Where he grew up, you learned to pick out the people with guts. The lady minister had plenty of guts. Too bad they weren't going to help her in the end.

" — do it."

"What?"

"I said to get it right this time. The reverend needs to be stopped."

"You said you didn't want her hurt, just scared."

"Never mind what I said. Just stop her. Any way you can."

"It'll cost you."

"I'm aware of that."

The boss was losing it. Tony didn't much mind. After all, as long as he got paid, it didn't matter one way or the other. He had other things to think about. Important things.

"When do I get my money?"

He almost chuckled at the angry hiss on the other end of the line. Funny how people used to being in charge didn't like being reminded that they had to pay up, just like everybody else. He was in the driver's seat. His chest expanded at the realization. No more people telling him what to do.

"You'll get it when the job's done."

"Uh-uh. Half now, half later."

"Listen, you little creep —"

"No, you listen. You want the lady taken care of, you do it my way. Otherwise, you get yourself another man."

"You're in no —"

"Careful."

"Okay, half now."

Tony almost laughed at the capitulation in the boss's voice. Once this job was done, he was getting out of here. Going somewhere warm. Tahiti sounded good. Or maybe somewhere in the Caribbean.

"I want half up front," he reminded the boss.

"You'll get it. Drop-off's the same as before."

"I'll be there."

The phone clicked. Tony recradled the receiver. Yeah, it felt good calling the shots. He grinned suddenly. A smart guy could do pretty well for himself if he was willing to take a chance. He figured he was a pretty smart guy.

He looked around his apartment — leaky pipes, stained ceilings, broken windows. He was meant for better things. In a couple of days, he was going to have them.

All he had to do was take out one little lady minister.

Life was good.

CHAPTER EIGHT

"Reverend Hastings?"

The voice was familiar, yet she couldn't place it.

"Reverend Hastings?" More insistent this time, the voice demanded her attention.

"Yes?"

"We've got something you want."

"Who is this?"

"That doesn't matter. You know that scarf you gave your husband? The blue one."

For the first time, she felt a tremor of fear. "What about it?"

"We've got it."

"So? Sam could have dropped it. Anyone could have picked it up." She ignored the fact that he'd had it with him when he left the house this morning.

"It's what we've got with it that ought to interest you."

She kept her voice cool. "Oh? And what's that?"

"Your husband."

"I don't believe you."

The caller laughed, and at last she placed him. Her assailant.

"Maybe you'd like to talk to him?" A pause. "If you ask real pretty, I just might let you."

She wouldn't play this game. Sam was at a council meeting. He'd called not an hour ago, saying he'd be home soon. Someone had obviously found out that he wasn't home and was playing mind games with her.

"Carla."

Sam's voice.

"Sam, where are you? Who's —"

"That's enough," the hateful voice interrupted. "Now do you believe me?"

"What do you want?"

"You." Another pause. "You come here and I'll let your husband go."

"What do you want with me?"

"To talk with you. Help you see reason about the warehouse. After that, I'll let both of you go."

"How do I know you're telling the truth?"

"Hey, preacher, you're not accusing me of lying, are you?" He laughed and she cringed, the rasping sound forcibly reminding her of an arm pressed to her neck, slowly choking the life out of her.

"Where and when do you want me?"

"That's better, lady." He rattled off an address. "Be there in thirty minutes. No later, or . . ." His voice trailed off suggestively.

"Wait. I don't know where that is."

"So take a cab."

The phone clicked.

Slamming the door on her imagination, she hung up and dialed the numbers of the city building. The call could still be a hoax. Maybe someone had obtained a tape recording of Sam's voice. Maybe . . . She waited impatiently until a voice announced, "City and County Building. May I help you?"

"Sam Hastings, please. City Council room."

"Just a moment."

A soft rock song crooned in her ears. Normally Carla didn't mind the music that filled the void of waiting. But tonight the love-gone-wrong tune only rankled against her already sensitized nerves.

"I'm afraid Mr. Hastings isn't here."

"Do you know when he left?"

A slightly annoyed "I'll check" left Carla waiting again. Waiting and praying.

"Mr. Hastings left the building thirty minutes ago."

"Thank you."

She checked her watch. It was not quite

seven-thirty. Sam would be home in a few minutes. She ignored the steady ticking of the clock and concentrated on the front door, willing it to open, praying Sam would be there. Five minutes passed. Ten. If she didn't call a cab soon, she'd be late.

By ten minutes to eight, she knew she couldn't wait any longer. Sam's life could depend on what she did in the next few minutes.

George nudged her legs, and she stooped to wrap her arms around his neck, needing the contact. After she let him lick her face, he trotted over to where his leash hung on the coat tree. He looked up at her expectantly.

"Sorry, boy," she said, standing and straightening her clothes. "You can't come this time."

She spared a minute to scribble a note. If this was all a hoax, she wanted Sam to know where she'd gone and why. If it wasn't . . . Well, if it wasn't, it wouldn't matter.

Sam needed her.

The taxi sloshed along the rain-slick streets. She watched as they passed respectable stores and shops, family-style restaurants, middle-class homes. Respectable gave way to shabby, shabby to rundown, until they entered the war zone of the city. No one came here unless they had to.

The cab pulled up in front of a bar, its neon lights casting a green and pink glow over the wet cement. Carla peered out the window and tried not to let her dismay show. A sign, hanging crookedly, announced the bar as JOE'S PLACE. She'd seen bars before, but never one this seedy. Even from a distance, she could register the apathetic looks on the faces of the few people brave — or foolhardy — enough to loiter outside.

The cabbie turned in his seat. "Sorry, ma'am. I ain't going no farther. You'll have to walk the rest of the way. It ain't far."

"I understand," she said, working to suppress the quiver in her voice. She pressed a couple of bills into his hand. "I don't suppose you'd wait —"

"Sorry," he repeated. "Ain't no amount of money that would make me hang around these parts. And, if you've got any sense, you'll let me take you back home. A lady like you ain't got no business here. And that's a fact."

"Thanks." She opened the door and climbed out, hesitating only briefly.

The cab sped away, its lights radiating tunnels of yellow through the night. She wanted to call it back, to climb in the smoke-filled interior, and do as the cabbie suggested. But she couldn't.

Once her eyes adjusted to the gloom of rain and darkness, relieved only by the one unbroken streetlight on the block, she looked about. And wished she hadn't. Naively she thought she'd been prepared for what she'd find. After all, she'd been in some of the worst neighborhoods in the city. She believed she'd seen the worst humanity had to offer.

She'd been wrong.

Broken glass littered what passed for sidewalks. Graffiti-scarred walls mocked the pocket-size yard of scraggly grass outside what once might have been a school. Furtive shadows loomed in doorways. From a window above her, a blaring television competed with the clamor of voices arguing, cursing, crying.

As repulsive as the surroundings were, it was the faces of the people who shambled along the street that tore at her heart. She was familiar with faces filled with despair and pain. As much as it hurt to look into the eyes of someone who'd known tragedy, she had dealt with it, helped when she could, offered comfort when it was needed. But the faces that she encountered now registered no pain, no grief, no despair, only apathy. A curious lack of emotion, as if they were beyond feeling, beyond help, beyond anything.

Male and female, young and old, the expressionless look in their eyes was the common denominator between them. Another time, another place, she'd have tried to reach these people whose souls appeared more empty than the abandoned buildings that lined the street. She could only say a silent prayer for them now.

Clutching her purse more tightly against her side, she started in what she hoped was the right direction, picking her way around empty bottles and cans, careful to stick close to the edge of the sidewalk. She recalled every tip she'd ever read about self-defense. Keep your eyes straight ahead. Don't look to the right or left. Don't register any reaction to the voices that called to her from darkened doorways. Above all, don't look afraid.

"Hey, baby, you looking for me?"

The taunting voice caused her steps to falter, but only for a moment. She mustered every scrap of courage she possessed and kept walking. Jeering laughter followed her.

Someone whistled, a shrill, penetrating sound that prompted her to reach inside her purse and fumble for her keys. Poking them through her fist so that the ends pointed out, she felt marginally better. It might not be much, but it was at least some protection. She closed her ears to the vulgarities shouted at her. She wanted to close her eyes to the ugliness that surrounded her, but blocking it out was a luxury she couldn't afford. She kept her eyes wide open and wept inside for the wasted lives that hid behind the voices that were even now screaming obscenities at her.

She didn't have to check the address she carried in her purse; she'd read it so many times that she'd memorized it. A car splashed along the street, splattering her shoes and stockings with cold, muddy water. She brushed ineffectually at them before giving it up as a lost cause.

Just when she'd determined that the cab driver had taken her to the wrong place, she saw it. The street number on it barely visible, the building looked like a site marked for demolition. Gaping holes replaced windows. Iron bars, ripped from their window settings, were mute evidence of failed attempts to secure the building.

She shivered, whether from cold or fear, she wasn't sure. She'd been an idiot to come here alone. But what choice did she have?

None.

Sam needed her. Nothing else mattered.

She wasn't surprised when the door opened as she pushed against it. A lock clicked shut behind her.

Tony watched as she let herself inside. He grinned. She'd played right into his hands. The boss was right. All it took was the proper motivation and you could get any-body to do anything. Even convince a proper little lady minister to come to the city's war zone — a four-block square that even the cops avoided.

He congratulated himself on making sure that the husband was out of reach. He'd figured she'd try to reach him. Tony had to hand it to the boss. Providing that little detail about the scarf convinced her he was telling the truth. Had he ever been that gull-ible? He didn't think so. He'd grown up knowing people lied as easily as they breathed. Too bad the lady minister hadn't learned the same lesson.

Still muttering about the wild goose chase he'd wasted the last hour on, Sam let himself in.

"Carla? I'm home. You wouldn't believe where I've been. Some crackpot called up, said he had information about the ware-house. Like a fool, I went to meet him. And

180

ended up waiting for forty-five minutes before I gave up."

He peeled off his gloves and started unbuttoning his coat when he realized there was no answer.

"Carla?"

George bounded into the room and jumped on Sam.

"Where's Carla?"

The dog cavorted around the room, his paws scraping against the hardwood floor.

Sam bent to scratch George behind the ears. "Where is she?" He straightened and headed to the kitchen. There, on the table, he saw the note.

What he read caused his blood to grow cold. "Carla, no." She wouldn't be so foolish as to go off on her own, not after he'd all but ordered her to bej careful. But even as he reassured himself, he knew better. His fury grew in direct proportion to his fear as he acknowledged that she'd done exactly that. How could she have done something so stupid?

On the heels of his anger came compre-hension. Carla believed he was in danger and had gone to help him. Would he have done any differently? The swiftness with which the answer came mocked his initial anger.

No.

He'd have done exactly the same thing.

He made the twenty-minute trip in ten, parked and locked his car, and prayed it would still be there when he returned. In this part of the city, he had little hope that particular prayer would be answered. He gave the possibility scant heed. Losing a car paled in comparison to losing Carla.

It was so clear that everything, from the smallest blade of grass to the silhouette of the buildings, was outlined in sharp detail against the sky. The recent rain had washed the air clean. Unfortunately it hadn't rid the streets of the filth that littered them. The air was still and so icy that his breath came in feathery puffs. His suit jacket was scant protection against the cold, and he huddled deeper into it. He scanned the buildings for an address. Street signs, if they ever existed, were long gone. The dingy storefronts, shattered windows, and litter-strewn sidewalks were mute evidence of a neighborhood that had given up.

Carla wouldn't give up. He almost smiled, thinking of how she'd see a challenge in the decay and wreckage. She'd mobilize the residents, help them see that their homes and lives were worth saving, and then she would do something about it. When she set her mind to something, nothing stopped her. He only prayed he'd have the chance to see her in action.

Since they'd been married, he'd developed a sixth sense that kicked in whenever she needed him. His intuition was now screaming inside his head. Carla was in trouble.

Carla banged on the door until her knuckles were bruised and bloody.

"Who's there?"

Only the sigh of the wind answered her.

"I know someone's there." She fought to keep the fear from her voice, but she was afraid it slipped through. Clamping the lid down on her growing panic, she tried again. "Who is it?"

She thought she heard a faint scuffle, but she couldn't be sure.

Encouraged, she tried again. "What good is keeping me here going to do? People will be looking for me."

Still no answer.

"Look, whoever you are, you don't scare me. Only a coward hides and doesn't show his face. And you won't win. The community home's going to be built no matter what. You can't stop it."

Again she heard a faint sound. It could have come from behind the door. Or it could have been her imagination going haywire. Right now she wasn't sure. She looked around for some kind of weapon. Her gaze landed on a pile of two-by-fours. She curled her fingers around one and held it in front of her.

She huddled in a corner, drew her coat around her, and prepared to wait. Her breath seemed to echo in the empty room, then tremble back to her on a wave. The effect was eerie. She tried to level her breathing until it was slow and even. Twenty minutes passed.

She was cold. Colder than she'd ever been in her life. She pulled herself up and began to pace. Twenty steps across the room. Twenty steps back. Twenty steps . . .

She paced until her legs were numb. Finally she could go on no more and sank to the floor. Her thoughts were muzzy and she tried to bring them into focus. Sam would be furious when he found she was gone. That was it. She'd think about Sam, think about how he could make her laugh with his foolishness, think about how he could make her feel warm and cherished with only a word, a gesture.

The cold was making her tired. So very

tired. She fought the weariness that wrapped its way around her, like a blanket too heavy to push away. Giving way to exhaustion was the worst thing she could do. Everything she'd ever read about hypothermia passed through her mind.

If she couldn't walk, she'd do what she could. Slowly she lifted her arms and forced them out in front of her, then drew them in. Out, then in. Strangely her arms didn't ache. She supposed she should be grateful for the cold. It had numbed her beyond registering pain — or anything else.

She was slipping . . . slipping into the darkness. There, maybe she'd be warm.

She awoke with a start at a sound.

Some of her exhaustion dropped away as fingers of fear curled around her.

"Who are you?"

The silence taunted her.

Anger slowly kindled within her. She welcomed it. At least it was something she could hang onto.

"Why don't you show yourself? Are you such a coward that you can't even face me?"

She thought she heard something. A stirring. Someone moving? Something? A horror movie she'd seen in her teens about giant rats came rushing back to her. She didn't mind mice. But rats were different.

She shuddered. She tried to remember everything she'd ever read about rats. Did they carry plague?

"Get a hold of yourself," she muttered impatiently. Rats. Plague. Obviously the cold hadn't numbed her imagination.

More out of frustration than any real thought that the door would open, she banged against it. To her astonishment, it gave way. Elated, she pushed it open. She found herself in a huge barnlike room. She ran to a set of double doors. The sound of footsteps from outside caused her to back away. Wildly she looked around for a hiding place. Before she could move, the door flew open.

Sam. She ran to him.

"You don't know how glad I am to see you." A look at his face made her stop. "I guess you're a little upset."

"I'm a lot upset. No. Make that furious." He grabbed her and pulled her to him. "You're all right?" he asked, running his hands over her.

"I'm fine. Now."

"He didn't hurt you?"

"I don't even know who it was."

"Come on. We're getting out of here."

The scraping of metal against wood

caused them to stop before running to the door.

"They've bolted the doors," Carla cried.

"It's no use," Sam said after they'd banged on the doors with no effect. They circled the room, looking for any means of escape. The windows were covered with wire mesh. "We might as well make ourselves comfortable." He sat down, propped his back against the wall, and pulled Carla close.

She nestled into the comforting warmth of his body, but she couldn't stop shivering.

Sam rubbed her arms through her coat. "You're freezing."

"Not anymore."

He rested his chin on top of her head. "When we get out of here, you and I are going to —" He paused and sniffed. "Do you smell something?"

She wrinkled her nose. "Gasoline. But where —"

"Look." He pointed to the smoke that was seeping under the door. "We've got to get out of here. Now."

Her gaze flew back to the windows. If they had some kind of tool, perhaps they could push the wire mesh aside and break the glass. Just as she was looking for something, the smoke erupted into flames.

The gasoline-fed fire spread quickly,

consuming whatever stood in its way. Flames soon engulfed the doorway.

"Keep down," Sam shouted.

Blue-white flames licked about them while smoke filled the air.

"Move!"

His shout served to paralyze her momentarily. She looked up to where a beam, weakened by the flames, teetered precariously. With a running tackle, Sam shoved Carla out of the way just as it crashed to the floor. She felt the rush of air as it narrowly missed her. A grunt of pain caused her to spin around. The beam had pinned Sam on the floor.

"My legs." He gasped. "I can't move."

"Sam!" When her efforts to lift the beam off him failed, she tried pulling him out from under it. Her eyes watered, and she swiped at them. She could barely make Sam out now. She reached for his hand, squeezed it, and leaned closer to hear his words over the roar of the fire.

"Get out of here."

She didn't bother answering. There was no way she was going to leave him.

Then she saw it. It wasn't much, a piece of metal pipe lying against the wall. She'd missed it earlier. She dropped to her hands and knees, groping her way across the floor to the west wall. Splinters bit into her hands, but she ignored the pain and focused all her energy on putting one hand in front of the other.

"Carla, get out of here."

Sam's voice, hoarse and raw, caused her to pause, but only for a moment. At last she reached the wall. Pushing herself up, she grabbed the pipe and began retracing her path. The smoke had thickened, stinging her eyes and scraping her throat. Only the thought of Sam trapped beneath the massive beam kept her going.

When she reached him, she realized she had to stop the flames that licked along the beam, sputtering and crackling. In minutes, they'd reach him. She jerked off her coat and began beating at them. They snapped and spit, sparks leaping from one spot to the next, but eventually she extinguished the fire. Temporarily. Positioning the pipe under the beam, she pushed on it with everything she had, ignoring the sting of the hot metal against her hands.

The beam didn't budge.

"It's no use," Sam said between gasps. He raised himself up on his elbows and pulled off his coat. "Put this over your head and get out of here. Before it's too late."

She tried again.

The beam moved. Only a few inches, but it was enough. It had to be.

"Sam, be ready," she shouted. She repeated the process, shifting all her weight onto the pipe and praying with all her might.

Sam inched his legs from beneath the wood. The pipe slipped, and she gripped it more tightly until he was completely free. Slipping her arms around his waist, she dragged him away from the blaze. Pausing to catch her breath, she calculated the distance to the wall of windows. At their present rate, they'd never make it. The fire was a greedy monster, destroying everything in its path.

She caught Sam under the arms and started pulling when he tugged at her hands.

"I can walk."

She helped him to his feet, wedged her shoulder under his arm, and braced herself to take his weight. Together they hobbled to the wall of windows. He reached for the pipe that she still clutched in her hand.

He swung at the mesh-covered glass. The wire bent enough so he could slip the pipe behind it and pry it loose. "Stand back." He waited until Carla had moved away before striking the window. It shattered, spraying him with shards of glass. He spread his jacket over the glass-encrusted ledge, boosted her up, and followed her out.

Outside, she gulped in cold air. "Are you all right?"

"Yeah." He pulled her into his arms and kissed her.

To his surprise, she pushed away and glared up at him. "Don't you ever do that again."

"What?" He looked at her, genuinely bewildered.

"Tell me to leave you." The anger in her voice was real, stopping him. "Do you honestly think I could have left you trapped there? Do you?"

"No."

Her face was soot-stained, her hair singed, her hands blistered. And she was beautiful. "You saved my life," he said, his voice not quite steady.

"You *are* my life." Tears, dark with dirt, streaked her face.

Gently he drew her to him again, careful not to touch her hands, and wiped her cheeks with a none-too-clean handkerchief. "And you are mine."

"Take care of those hands, young lady," the doctor in the emergency room said.

"Thanks. I will."

"They're going to hurt like crazy in a

couple of hours."

She smiled wryly. "I sort of figured that."

"Maybe this will help." He handed her a small brown bottle and scribbled some instructions on a notepad.

"Thanks again."

Her hands bandaged, she felt clumsy and slow as she tried to sign the forms necessary for her release.

Coming up behind her, Sam gently nudged her aside. "I'll do that."

"How are your legs?"

He gave a wry smile. "Nothing's broken. Just bruised."

She let him take care of the formalities and sank back on a couch while she waited. Her hands hadn't started to hurt yet. Maybe the doctor was wrong. She'd experience a little twinge and that would be the end of it.

Three hours later, she was ready to admit he'd been right. But she wasn't ready to take the pain medication. The label listed drowsiness as one of the possible side effects. And she couldn't afford that. Not right now. She had too much to do.

"Here," Sam said, holding two pills in one hand and a glass of water in the other.

"Not yet."

"Now."

"Sam, I've got Sunday's sermon to finish, a report for the youth committee to write, a couple of letters to the housing authority —"

"They can wait."

"But —"

"Your hands are hurting, aren't they?"

Reluctantly she nodded. "A little."

He studied her face. "Try a lot."

"Okay. They hurt a lot."

"Was that so hard to admit?"

"Yeah." Seeing the stubborn set to his lips, she popped the pills in her mouth, then made a face at him. "Satisfied?" She picked up her sermon, intending to add the finishing touches.

"I will be as soon as you're in bed where you belong."

"Just let me finish —"

He took the papers from her. "Later."

George laid his paws on her lap.

"Tell him, George," Carla said. "Tell him that I don't need to be babied."

George trotted over to the foot of the stairs, barked twice, and waited.

"Traitor," she grumbled. "Okay, okay, I'm going. But I'm not going to forget this."

Sam winked at the dog.

Ten minutes later she was in bed, quietly fuming about all that needed to be done.

George stuck his face in hers. She couldn't help but laugh at the concerned expression in his brown eyes.

Sam was standing over her. "You'll thank me for this tomorrow."

"Yeah?"

He bent down to kiss her. "Yeah."

Her annoyance melted at the love in his eyes. "I'm glad you're here."

"So am I, sweetheart."

She nestled into the pillows. He watched her fight sleep, then relax and eventually yield to its sweet embrace.

George, who'd taken his customary spot at the foot of the bed, looked up as Sam walked to the door.

"Take care of her, George."

A couple of hours later, Sam sighed deeply and massaged the back of his neck with one hand while he continued to punch keys with the other. Hours spent at the computer yielded no new facts. He'd fed in every scrap of information he had concerning the warehouse, the surrounding property, and the people most likely to benefit if the warehouse remained abandoned. The result was a big fat zero. Frustration gnawed at his gut as he acknowledged he was no nearer to unraveling the mystery than he had been weeks ago.

He wandered into the kitchen and downed a glass of orange juice, the cold drink soothing his throat, which was still raw and scratchy from the fire. He thought of the two hours he'd just put in at the computer and swore softly. There had to be *something.* Some reason why that warehouse was so important to someone. Unlike embezzlement or other corporate crimes, there was no paper trail to follow. Fowler had owned the warehouse for twenty years.

Given enough time, Sam didn't doubt he'd be able to solve the riddle. But time was a luxury he didn't have. Every instinct told him that things were coming to a head. Soon. That meant Carla was in more danger than ever.

"You fool."

"It wasn't my fault —" Tony's words were cut off in a spate of abuse.

His lips tightened as he listened to the boss call him every name in the book. He didn't have to take this. He'd done what he'd been ordered to. He'd planned it right down to the last detail. Was it his fault that the gutsy little reverend and her husband had managed to find their way out of the building?

His hand cramped around the phone.

"You want it done, you do it."

"You sniveling excuse of a man —"

Tony slammed the phone down. He'd had enough. With what he'd saved from his last couple of jobs, he could take off. He wasn't sticking around while the boss tried to take out the minister. Things were going sour. He could smell it. Yeah, that's what he'd do. Take off. No one told Tony Owens what to do. Never again.

CHAPTER NINE

"Carla, call for you," Tom called.

Carla dried her hands on the dish towel in the shelter's kitchen and reached for the phone Tom held. "Hello."

"Reverend Hastings?" The voice was vaguely familiar, and Carla tried to place it.

"Yes?"

"It's Sarah. Sarah Barclay at Horace Fowler's office."

"Oh, yes, Ms. Barclay."

"I got this number from your answering machine. I hope it's all right to call you there?"

"Of course it is."

An embarrassed laugh came over the phone. "I almost didn't call you, but . . ."

"Can I help you with something?"

A relieved sigh whispered over the line. "If only you would. It's Mr. Fowler. He's threatening to fire me. After twenty years. It's my own fault. I know it. You told me not to, but you were so nice and —"

"Ms. Barclay . . . Sarah . . . what happened?"

"I talked to him about the warehouse. He started shouting at me, calling me terrible names." She sniffled.

"How can I help?"

"If you could talk to him, tell him that I was only trying to help your group, it might persuade him to change his mind."

"I'd be happy to talk with Mr. Fowler for you, but I really don't think he'll change his mind. Especially for me."

"But he respects you," Sarah said. "He told me so after your appointment."

"He did?"

"Oh, yes. He respects people who stand up to him. He can't abide a yes-man."

Carla listened with growing amazement. That didn't sound like the Mr. Fowler she'd met. Maybe it had been a bad day for him. Maybe . . .

"Will you help me?"

How could she refuse? "Of course. When —"

"If you wouldn't mind, maybe you could drop by tonight? Say around six?"

Carla pulled the curtains to the side, looking uneasily at the steady fall of snow. The roads were certain to be icy by six o'clock.

Still, how could she refuse when Sarah was in the predicament simply because she'd tried to help her?

"I'll be there."

"Thank you. Thank you. I don't know what else to say."

"It's not necessary —"

"Oh, but it is. Maybe I can still do something to help you. After we clear up this mess —"

"Why don't we talk about it later?"

"You're right, of course. I'll see you at six."

Carla was still holding the phone long after Sarah had hung up. Something seemed off-kilter. Carla frowned, trying to decide what was bothering her about the conversation. Her imagination must have gone into overdrive.

"All right if I take off a little early?" she asked Tom.

"Sure. Anything wrong?"

She shook her head. "No. Just a friend who needs some help."

"You spend too much time running around helping others."

She grimaced. "You sound like Sam. Besides, look who's talking." Her gaze took in the overcrowded shelter.

Tom gave a sheepish smile. "Okay. You got me on that one." He cast a look out the window and whistled. "You sure you want to go out in this weather?"

"No, but I don't have much choice." She checked her watch. "If I'm going to get there by six, I'd better leave."

The roads were worse than she'd feared. When she reached Fowler's office, she heaved a sigh of relief.

She knocked lightly on the office door. "Ms. Barclay? Sarah?"

The door opened quickly. "Oh, Reverend Hastings. Thank you for coming."

The older woman practically gushed her appreciation, causing Carla to smile uncomfortably. "It's the least I could do after you tried to help me."

Sarah dabbed at her eyes. "I just don't know what I'd do if I lost this job. I've been here for twenty years. It's the only thing I know."

Carla patted Sarah's shoulder. "I know. If we can't straighten this out with Mr. Fowler, I'll help you find something else."

"Would you?"

"Of course. Maybe Sam knows of something. He has a lot of contacts."

Sarah checked her watch. "We'd better get going. The boss hates people to be late."

Carla looked around, noting the darkened inner office for the first time. "Aren't we meeting him here?"

"He asked if I'd bring you to his house. I hope you don't mind. . . ."

Carla thought about the worsening weather and the snow-covered streets, which were bound to get worse as the temperature dropped. "No, I don't mind," she said, hoping she'd be forgiven for the small lie. "Where does he live?"

"Not far from here," Sarah said, pulling on her coat.

They took the elevator to the underground parking garage. Yellow-green fluorescent lights illuminated the garage. Carla glanced at her companion and recoiled slightly. Sarah's face was bathed in an eerie glow. A trick of light, nothing more, Carla assured herself. Still, she couldn't help the reflex that caused her to pull her coat more tightly around her.

"Would you like me to drive, dear?" Sarah asked.

"That's all right," Carla said. "I'll take it slow."

"But I know the way. I think it would be better if I drove. That way you can think about what you want to say to Mr. Fowler."

It made sense, and Carla handed her keys to Sarah, trying not to stare at the woman's face, which was still awash in the fluorescent light. She slid in the passenger side and buckled the seat belt around her. "You're familiar with a stick shift?"

Sarah wedged her plump body behind the wheel. "I grew up on my daddy's farm. If it's got four wheels and an engine, I can drive it." She laughed and pushed the seat back a notch. "Too many danishes."

Sarah pulled out of the garage and headed north. They steadily picked up speed, leaving the business district behind. Sarah handled the car competently, but Carla cringed inwardly as they slipped and slid over the icy streets. She glanced at Sarah, but the older woman didn't seem disturbed about the condition of the roads or inclined to decrease her speed.

To get her mind off images of grisly accidents, Carla looked out the window. She was surprised as they left the city limits. "I thought you said Mr. Fowler didn't live far away."

Sarah flashed a smile. "He doesn't."

The car skidded, careening crazily across the street. Carla held her breath as Sarah grappled with the steering wheel. She shouldn't have worried, though. Sarah handled the skid like a pro. She patted Carla's hand. "Just sit back and relax. I'll get us there in no time."

The older woman kept up a steady stream of small talk, probably, Carla decided, to help her relax. But she couldn't help noticing the passing scenery. With every mile they drove farther away from the city until they were in one of the surrounding suburbs.

"Where are we going?"

Sarah's smile was barely visible in the dark interior of the car. "You'll see."

Carla's uneasiness grew. "Maybe we should turn around. Come back when the weather's better."

"You're not worried, are you?"

"A little," Carla hedged.

"It's not much farther."

Sarah drove down a street of modest houses and pulled into a shrub-lined driveway. The house looked like any other in the neighborhood, with nothing to distinguish it from a thousand similar ones. It was well kept, but no more so than its neighbors. It didn't look like a house belonging to the owner of a multimillion-dollar business, but, Carla reminded herself, Fowler's office was hardly what she'd expected either. She climbed out of the car and followed Sarah as she walked inside.

"Make yourself at home," Sarah called, walking into the kitchen. "Mr. Fowler should be here any time."

Carla looked about. The house didn't look like it belonged to a man who lived alone. There were crocheted doilies on the room's high-backed chairs and sofa, women's magazines were arranged on a coffee table, silk flowers graced the mantel.

Sarah returned and pressed a cup of tea into Carla's hand. "Have some tea, dear. You're all tensed up. It'll help you relax."

"Thank you."

"I always say that there's nothing like a cup of tea to cure what ails you."

She was relaxed, just as Sarah had promised. And warm. Carla yawned and clamped a hand to her mouth. "Excuse me. I don't know why I'm so tired all of a sudden." She struggled to remember what they'd been talking about. Relaxing. That was it. "I find knitting helps me relax."

Sarah smiled. "That was a beautiful scarf you made for your husband. I always say blue is so becoming on a man."

"Thank you." Carla frowned. Something was bothering her. Something about the scarf. "How did you . . ." She yawned again and felt a strange lethargy overtake her. Her head felt heavy. What had she been about to say? Something about the scarf. She couldn't keep hold of the thought. She looked up to find Sarah watching her closely.

The man on the phone had mentioned the scarf. How had he known about it? Pieces started fitting together . . . if only she could hold on to them.

"The tea . . ." Half awake, half asleep, she heard Sarah laugh, a shrill sound that sent whispers of fear skittering down Carla's spine. She felt herself slipping into blackness.

Sam rubbed his eyes and stared at the report in front of him. The words still blurred around the edges. No amount of squinting or adjusting the angle of the paper helped.

"Better pack it up, Hastings," he muttered. When he couldn't even see to read, he knew he'd had enough. He cast one last look at the desk he occupied in the City Council offices. With no regret, he swept the papers into the top drawer. There'd be heck to pay tomorrow when the secretary saw the fiasco. He'd worry about that then. Right now he needed to make sure Carla was all right.

She'd called several hours ago to say she'd be at the shelter. He'd swing by on his way home and pick her up. They could get her car tomorrow morning. He knew he wasn't fooling her, but so far she'd been co-operative with his efforts to protect her. He also knew that if she decided someone needed her, she'd forget all about her own safety.

The warehouse wasn't far from the shelter. Maybe he'd stop there, see if things were quiet. Pulling into the rutted parking lot, he stared at the old building, starkly outlined in the glare of his headlights. Sighing, he climbed out of the car. He didn't even know why he was here. Only that he needed answers and was rapidly running out of places to look.

A bit of paper caught his attention. He stooped to pick it up and squinted at the scrap, trying to make out the words. It said TRI-CHEM. Tri-Chem Industries was one of the biggest handlers of chemical waste in the state. As far as he knew, though, they didn't have any treatment plants in the city. So what was one of their labels doing here in the parking lot of an abandoned ware-house? He stuffed the paper into his pocket and got back in his car.

Traffic moved in fits and starts as com-muters fought their way home through the snow-covered streets. Sam drummed his fingers on the steering wheel, waiting for the snarl of cars to ease, frowning over the label in his pocket.

At last he pulled up in front of the shelter. He scanned the street for Carla's car. When he didn't see it, he wasn't particularly surprised. She often parked in the alley behind the shelter, which doubled as a minuscule lot for the staff and volunteers.

Inside, he scanned the room for her. His gaze settled on Tom. "Where's Carla?"

Tom looked up from where he was filling out reports. "She got a call about an hour ago. Said a friend needed to see her."

"Did she happen to say who it was?"

Tom shook his head. "Is something wrong?"

"No." Sam forced a smile to his lips. "Nothing's wrong. I just thought I'd give her a ride home."

"Tell Carla thanks again when you see her. She was a lifesaver tonight."

"I will," Sam called over his shoulder.

He drove as fast as he dared. There was no reason to believe she wasn't all right. No reason for the hair at the nape of his neck to prickle. No reason except for a feeling in his gut that told him Carla was in trouble.

By the time he turned onto their street, he'd managed to convince himself he had overreacted. Carla had gone to help a friend. She'd be at home waiting for him, they'd make some hot chocolate, and . . .

Her car wasn't there.

That didn't mean anything, he assured himself. Still, he had barely cut the engine when he jumped out of the car and ran to the house. He fumbled with his keys, the cold metal stinging his hands as he tried to unlock the door.

George greeted him with a hungry bark.

Automatically Sam stooped to pet the dog. "Okay, boy. Let me check the answering machine first, and then it's chow time."

George barked his agreement.

Sam pressed the playback button.

"Carla, it's Maude. You and Sam remember you're coming for Sunday dinner. We're having . . ." He hit the fast-forward button. "Reverend, it's Porter. The church's toilet has overflowed again. Had to call a plumber." Impatiently Sam fast-forwarded through the message and several others. It seemed everyone in the congregation had called. Everyone but Carla.

George nudged Sam's leg.

"Okay, I'm coming." He filled George's dish.

When the phone rang, Sam jumped to answer it. "Carla?"

"Sam, it's Tom. Did Carla get home all right?"

Sam didn't bother to keep the disappointment from his voice. "Not yet."

"I shouldn't have let her go."

"You couldn't have stopped her," Sam said, knowing it was true.

"Would you give me a ring when she gets in?" Tom asked.

"Sure. Thanks for calling."

Sam hung up the phone with relief. He wanted the line clear. The shrill of the doorbell made him jump up.

Jared stood there. "You were going to teach me some chess moves."

Sam groaned. He'd completely forgotten. "This isn't a real good time, Jared. Maybe another time —" The look on the boy's face forced him to reconsider. He couldn't do anything except wait. Waiting with someone beat waiting alone.

"Okay." Sam pulled the chess board out of a cabinet and gestured for Jared to start setting up the pieces, all the while willing the phone to ring.

"You're sure you want to do this?" Jared asked.

Sam summoned a smile. "Sure I'm sure."

"Checkmate," Jared crowed an hour later. "That's twice in a row."

"Uh, yeah. Congratulations." Sam looked at the phone, willing it to ring. It remained stubbornly silent.

When it rang, he grabbed for it. "Carla?"

"Hastings, Horace Fowler here."

Sam was in no mood to listen to Fowler's excuses about why he couldn't sell the warehouse. "Mr. Fowler, this isn't a good time. Could I call you back? Tomorrow maybe?"

"Listen, Hastings. You've been after me to sell the warehouse to the City for two months. Now I want to sell it and you say this isn't a good time?"

"You want to sell the warehouse?" Sam asked, wanting to make sure he'd heard correctly.

"You heard me."

"That's . . . uh . . . great." Sam checked his watch before dragging his attention back to what Fowler was saying.

". . . kept telling me I ought to hang on to the place, but —"

"I'm sorry," Sam interrupted. "Could you say that again?"

Fowler's grunt of impatience came loudly across the line. "Sarah. My secretary suggested I keep the place as a tax write-off, but —"

"Sarah Barclay convinced you not to sell?"

"That's what I said."

"But . . ." Sam tried to remember what Carla had told her about the woman. His own meeting with Sarah had been so brief, he didn't remember much about her, only enough to notice she pretty much faded into the background. "What caused you to change your mind?"

"My daughter got into town this evening. When she heard about the warehouse and what you intend to do with it, she said I'd better get off my duff and do what's right."

"That's great."

"Well, you don't sound very happy about it," Fowler grumbled.

"Sorry. My wife hasn't come home yet and I'm a little worried about her."

"What's that?"

"Carla. She's not home yet."

"I saw her leave the office with Sarah not an hour ago. Don't know why they were going off together, but I figured it wasn't any of my business."

"Carla was at your office?"

"Didn't I just say that?" Fowler harumphed. "You young folks just don't listen. Saw her and Sarah leave together. I'd already left, but I discovered I'd left my gloves back in the office. I saw them just as they were getting into the elevator."

Sam tried to digest what Fowler had told him.

"I'll sign the bill of sale and send it to you tomorrow."

"What . . . oh . . . thanks."

With another harumph, Fowler hung up.

Sam replaced the phone. Why had Sarah Barclay tried to prevent the sale of the warehouse? And what, if anything, did it have to do with the Tri-Chem label he'd found in the parking lot?

He picked up the phone. "Tom, it's Sam. Was the friend who called Carla a woman?"

"Yeah. Is it important?"

"It might be," Sam said, not bothering to say goodbye. He pulled some bills from his wallet, then stashed them in Jared's hand. "Take a cab home, all right?"

"What's going on?"

Fear was gnawing at his gut, and Sam bit back the sharp words that hovered on the tip of his tongue. "I have to find Carla."

"I want to go with you."

"I don't have time for this." Sam stopped himself and looked at the boy, whom he'd come to love. He saw the fear in Jared's eyes. But he saw something more as well. Concern. If Sam hadn't been scared out of his mind, he'd have smiled, thinking of Carla's reaction to the change in Jared. She'd been praying that Jared's sense of compassion for others would awaken. And it had. If only she were here to share it with him.

Jared laid his hand on Sam's arm. "I can help. Please."

Touched by the sincerity in the boy's voice, Sam closed his hand on Jared's shoulder. "Thanks for the offer. But I can't let you go with me."

"You think I'm just a kid, don't you?"

"You *are* a kid," Sam said gently. "If anything happened to you, I'd be responsible."

"I can take care of myself." Jared slid Sam an embarrassed look. "Besides, if Carla's in trouble, I want to help."

"Right now the best thing you can do is go home."

"Okay."

Sam looked at the boy in surprise. He hadn't expected such an easy capitulation, but he didn't have time to wonder about it.

"You find Carla. I'll get myself home," Jared said.

"Thanks." Sam picked up the phone, dialed a number, and waited, praying he was wrong.

CHAPTER TEN

"Don't know what couldn't have kept till morning," Fowler muttered.

Sam was already scanning the office. "Where would Sarah be likely to keep something she doesn't want anyone else to see?"

Fowler scowled. "Sarah doesn't have any secrets. Why, the woman's been with me for more than twenty years. She's as plain as a fence post, but she's a good secretary."

Sam wasn't paying attention. Carla was missing and the only lead he had was Fowler's secretary. How Sarah Barclay figured in the warehouse mess, he didn't know.

He started pulling out drawers from the bank of file cabinets lining one wall. Sarah's files were meticulously kept. They yielded nothing out of the ordinary. He slammed a drawer shut, his gaze settling on the computer.

"Who else uses the computer besides Sarah?"

"No one."

"Not even you?"

"Don't much like these newfangled machines," Fowler said, looking embarrassed.

Sam flicked the power switch and waited for the menu to appear. He punched on some keys, bringing up the file directory. Business letters, contracts, proposals. Everything appeared in order, but then he hadn't expected to find what he was looking for in the regular files.

He needed the code word. Most people chose something familiar. Fowler dug out Sarah's employment records, and Sam tried her birth date, social security number, even her driver's license number. Swearing softly, he started all over again, methodically reversing the order of the numbers. When he found it, he marveled at the simplicity of the code, HARAS — Sarah spelled backward.

He scrolled through the file, whistling at what he found. For the past fifteen years the warehouse had served as a transfer site for hundreds of companies wanting to get rid of industrial waste without paying the cost. It was all there. Names, dates, amounts.

His mouth tightened as he quickly esti-
mated the amount of hazardous waste
dumped illegally all over the state. Sarah's
ingenuity was exceeded only by her ar-
rogance in keeping the files in the office
under Fowler's nose. The warehouse was
valuable only as long as the area remained
undeveloped.

"What is it?" Fowler demanded.

Sam left the computer on. "See for
yourself."

Carla awoke, her head groggy and woozy.
She could have been asleep for minutes . . .
or hours. Her hands were tied behind her
back with some kind of tape. She looked
down to find her ankles bound also. She
wriggled her fingers experimentally.

"It won't do you any good."

Sarah was sitting across the living room,
watching her, just as she had before Carla
had dozed off. She held a gun in her hand,
trained on Carla.

"You put something in the tea." Carla
tried to ignore the horrifying sight of the
weapon.

The older woman smiled complacently.
"Just a little something to put you to sleep
while I decided what to do."

"What to do?"

216

"With you. I couldn't just let you go around asking questions and stirring up trouble, now could I? If only you'd listened to the nice warnings I sent." Sarah shook her head regretfully. "But you didn't."

Carla looked at Sarah. This wasn't the woman she'd met in Fowler's office. Her eyes were hard, the laugh lines around her mouth were now deep grooves, even the comfortable plumpness of her figure seemed to have taken on a stiff, harsh line.

"It was you all along, wasn't it?"

"Of course it was me. You don't think Fowler could have pulled this off, do you? Who do you think ran the business all these years? Fowler? He couldn't find his way out of the men's room without help."

Sarah laughed contemptuously. "He's stupid, cheap, and boringly honest. It was me. Me. I did it all. Right under his nose."

Carla heard a boastful tone in Sarah's voice that revealed a sick kind of pride.

"But how . . . Didn't Mr. Fowler mind, you taking over the business?"

"Mind? He doesn't have the brains to mind. He thinks he's the one who turned Fowler Industrial into one of the biggest players in the city."

"And you —"

"I let him believe it. It suited both our purposes."

"But why? Why not start your own business?"

"Do you know what it was like for a woman twenty years ago? Of course not. You were scarcely out of diapers then. A woman couldn't get financing for her own business. No banker would even talk to me about a small loan, much less one big enough to start up my own company. It takes money to start a business. Lots of money. That was the one thing I didn't have. So I wangled a job as Fowler's secretary."

"Why Fowler?"

"He's a fool. He was even a bigger fool back then. He thought he had the brains to run the company himself. Now he knows he can't do it without me.

It was hard going at first, finding ways to turn a buck on the side, but then the EPA started with all their rules and regulations. It was perfect. A lot of companies didn't want to fork over all their profits to get rid of chemical waste."

"So you provided them with a dump site."

"The warehouse isn't the dump site."

"Then why were you trying to scare us off?"

"It's our way station. Companies bring

whatever they need to get rid of to the warehouse. We take care of it for them." Sarah smiled, her teeth gleaming. "You and me — you could say we're in the same business." At Carla's confused look, Sarah added, "We're both in the service industry. We just go about it differently."

Carla's fear grew as she saw the sparkle in Sarah's eyes. Sarah looked as if she honestly believed what she was saying.

She had to keep Sarah talking. "You couldn't have done it all by yourself."

"You're right. I hired a couple of jerks with more muscles than brains. They're smart enough to do what they're told and not to ask any questions."

"Where do you take the stuff?"

"Different places. Right now the boys are taking it to a ravine out in the country."

"You dump hazardous waste, knowing what it will do to the land?"

"People are going to do what they want to. I just make it easy for them. They don't have to worry about where the stuff goes, and we all get rich. It's a perfect setup. Or it was. The warehouse has been abandoned for years, a leftover from Fowler's father's time. The whole block was vacant. Nobody paid attention to what we were doing. Until you and your fancy uptown husband came along stirring everything up.

"We had to stop when people started moving back into the area. Too many people asking questions."

"So you threatened Jack Thompson?"

Sarah snorted. "He was stupid. I would have paid him ten times what his crummy little fix-it shop was worth. But, no, he had to hold on to it. That's why I had Tony pay him a little visit."

"Tony?"

"You know Tony." Sarah smiled slyly. "He came to see you not long ago."

Carla shivered, remembering the stench of his breath, the feel of his arm clamped around her neck as she gasped for air.

Sarah nodded in satisfaction. "I see you remember him. He also arranged that little welcome party for you a few nights ago."

"The fire?"

"Yeah. I knew how to make sure you came. I told him about that blue scarf you made for your husband. I find details like that add so much to making a good plan, don't you?" Sarah preened with self-satisfaction.

"How did you get a recording of Sam's voice?"

"One of the secretaries for the City Council is a friend of mine. I told her I needed it for a practical joke I was playing on my boss. All it took was a little editing and I had the perfect bait." She flicked Carla a scornful glance. "You played right into our hands. So touching — all that wifely concern for your husband. Do you think he'd have done the same for you?" she asked, not giving Carla a chance to respond. "No way. Men are only out for what they can get.

"Take Tony. He thinks he can blackmail me — I could see it in his eyes the last time we met." Sarah gave a cackling laugh. "I made sure he can never tie anything to me. If he tries to give the police anything, it'll come right back to him. And who are they going to believe? A two-bit loser with a record a mile long or a responsible citizen like me?

Tony's stupid even for a man, but then that's what I wanted. I stumbled on him almost by accident. I was looking for someone who wasn't afraid to get his hands dirty and found an underground rag called *Dirty Deeds*. Tony was answering phones. Can you believe it? He jumped at the chance to make some real money."

Even talking about Tony made Carla's skin crawl. She directed the conversation back to the warehouse. "Why didn't Fowler ever sell the warehouse?"

"I convinced him to hold on to it, told him it could be worth a lot more when the rest of the block was built up." She glared at Carla. "Everything would have been fine if you'd just minded your own business."

"The community home is everyone's business."

"Get real, Reverend. No one but a few do-gooders like you cares about it. If it hadn't been for you, the whole idea would have died."

"So you decided to scare me off."

"Yeah. I have to hand it to you, you don't scare easy," Sarah said with grudging respect. "I thought for sure you'd give up after I had your church vandalized." She grinned slyly. "Did you like our little greetings?"

Carla looked at the older woman in horror.

"Don't look at me like that."

"Like what?"

"Like I'm crazy."

"I feel sorry for you," Carla said. "You've let your greed take over your life."

"Do you know what it's like to be poor? So poor that you never even knew what a store-bought dress looked like? So poor that you counted yourself lucky if you got half a potato to eat at night? I do. I grew up that way. My old man scratched a living out of the dirt until it killed him. When I was old enough to leave home, I promised myself I was never going to be poor again."

For a moment, Carla forgot about the threats, the gun, the twisted expression on Sarah's face. She saw only a frightened child who'd grown up hungry and poor. "Let me help you."

"I don't want your help. I don't need it. I'm rich. Richer than you can ever imagine. And all because I wasn't afraid to take risks. That's what's wrong with most women. They end up in dead-end jobs or married to some slob who treats them like dirt." She smiled bitterly. "I ought to know."

"You were married?"

"If you want to call it that. I prefer to think of it as bondage. I divorced him and never looked back."

"Sarah, let me help you. If we explain —"

"Explain what? That I helped companies dump their waste illegally?" She shook her head. "I'm not explaining anything. I won't have to."

"But they'll find out. I'll tell them."

"You really are a naive little fool, aren't you? Do you honestly think I'm going to let you go?"

Carla hadn't let herself think about it.

Now she had no choice. "What are you going to do with me?"

"You're going to have an accident. Nobody will be more shocked than I am when your car runs off the road on a bridge not far from here. Such a tragedy. But with these slick roads, well . . . accidents do happen."

Carla forced the picture Sarah had painted from her mind. Sam would already know she was missing. He'd find her.

"He can't help you."

"Who?"

"Your precious Sam. You think I don't know what you're thinking? Your face gives you away."

"You haven't hurt anyone yet," Carla said, trying to keep the panic from her voice. "Why don't you let me go?"

Sarah laughed again. "Let you go? You almost ruined everything. You with your highfalutin ideas about a community home. You wouldn't listen. You and that fancy husband of yours. You had your chance. Now it's too late."

"It's not too late. Not yet. But if you hurt me —"

"Anyone ever tell you that you talk too much?" Sarah pulled a roll of duct tape from her pocket. Cutting a piece off, she placed it over Carla's mouth. "There."

It should have been a peaceful scene, Sam reflected. There was nothing here to cause the hairs at the nape of his neck to prickle with uneasiness. Nothing to send his heart-beat into overdrive, nothing to make his mouth go dry . . . nothing but a sick cer-tainty that Carla was inside with a woman who'd already proved she was totally ruth-less.

The quiet neighborhood was postcard-pretty with its neatly painted houses, well-kept yards, and freshly shoveled sidewalks. Children sledded down a bank, their squeals breaking the silence of the otherwise still morning. The house he was looking for ap-peared no different than its neighbors. Smoke curled from the chimney while a stack of wood flanked the side. A cat lounged in the front window.

He drove by slowly, as if looking for an address. The garage door was closed. He didn't pause but kept driving until he reached the end of the block. There he parked his car and doubled back on foot. Grateful for the early-morning mist that provided some cover, he kept to the shad-ows. When he neared the house, he ducked behind a hedge and crept along the side of the house. Peering into the garage window, he found what he was looking for.

Carla's car.

It was what he'd been hoping for. Still, the sight of it caused his breath to lodge in his throat. Impatiently he tamped down his fear. There'd be time enough for that later. Now he needed to think. Carla's life depended on what he did in the next few minutes.

Sarah Barclay knew him. He couldn't just barge in. She could kill Carla before he could stop her. There had to be another way. A sound behind him made him whirl around. He had his arm clamped around someone's neck before he realized who it was.

"Jared." Sam dropped his arm.

"Yeah," Jared said in a squeaky voice. "That was some move. You gotta show it to me sometime."

"What I want to do is wring your neck. How did you get here anyway?"

"Easy. I climbed in the backseat when you were on the phone."

Sam glared at the boy, who matched him stare for stare.

"Hey, man, it's cool."

"What are you doing here?"

"I thought you might need some help."

Sam was torn between wanting to shake some sense into Jared and give him a bear hug. Maybe later. Right now, he had to get into the house. And Jared might just be the ticket inside.

"Can you do exactly what I say?"

"You bet."

"Then here's what we're going to do."

From his position behind a screen of shrubs, Sam watched as Jared walked up the sidewalk, a morning newspaper he'd filched from a neighbor's yard in hand. He listened for the rap.

"Good morning, ma'am. I'm here to offer you a subscription to the *Post* with a complimentary copy of today's paper."

The voice that answered him was annoyed. *Good.* That meant Sarah was rattled.

As Sam had instructed, Jared pushed the door open a little wider. "If I could just come in and tell you about the offer, I'm sure —"

"Not today." Sarah started to close the door.

"I only need one more subscription to win a trip to Washington, D.C.," Jared wheedled.

Sam pried open an old-fashioned window and lowered himself inside a bedroom. He padded across the room and eased open a door. His pulse went into overdrive when he saw Carla trussed up on the sofa. Gently he peeled the tape from her mouth. "Did she hurt you?"

"N-no. Sam, she's crazy. She's been using the warehouse to —"

"I know," he said, freeing her arms and legs. "Come on. I'm getting you out of here."

The cock of a gun hammer had him whirling around. He found Sarah with a revolver trained on them.

He put Carla behind him. "It's all over, Sarah."

The woman leveled the gun at his chest. "Try again."

Sam directed his gaze over her shoulder. "Maybe you should look behind you."

She laughed. "You must really think I'm a fool."

"No. Anything but."

"Drop it, lady."

The surprise on Sarah's face was almost comical as she dropped the gun. Almost. Sam could easily have wrung Jared's neck. He might still do it. Later. After he'd dealt with Sarah. He picked up the gun and aimed it at her.

"I told you to stay outside," he said to Jared.

"Thought you might need some backup,"

the boy said, holding up the chess piece he'd pressed into Sarah's back.

Sam groaned, still keeping the gun on Sarah. "Call 911."

It had been two days since Sarah Barclay's arrest. In spite of everything, Carla couldn't help but feel sorry for the woman. Her greed had caused her to waste her life.

George plopped his paws on Carla's lap and licked her face.

"I know, you're waiting for Sam too, aren't you?" She scratched his neck and checked her watch for the third time in the last ten minutes.

Sam had received a call early that morning. When she'd asked who it was, he'd only smiled mysteriously and promised she'd know soon enough.

When she heard the key being turned, she ran to the door. "Give," she demanded.

He grinned. "Miss me, did you?"

"Where did you go? Did it have anything to do with the warehouse? What's going to happen to Sarah and Tony Owens? What —"

He held up a hand. "The police picked up Tony today. He was only too eager to spill his guts. He and Sarah are so eager to blame each other, the DA's going to have more

229

than enough evidence to put them both away for a long time."

She shuddered, and Sam folded her into his arms. "They can't hurt you anymore."

"What about the warehouse?"

"Did you know the Environmental Protection Agency has an office right here in the city? They were very interested to learn about Sarah's little extracurricular activities."

"Sam Hastings, if you don't tell me about the warehouse, so help me —"

"The EPA will have to do some testing, but there doesn't appear to have been any leakage. Once the warehouse gets a clean bill of health, we'll start building."

"You mean —"

"I mean we're going to have a community home."

She wrapped her arms around his neck. "Anyone ever tell you that you're wonderful?"

"Not lately."

"Then I'll just have to prove it, won't I?"

EPILOGUE

Carla pushed open the door of the model apartment in the community home and gave a little cry of excitement. "It's beautiful, Sam. Just like I pictured."

Shafts of sunlight streamed in through snowy white curtains, highlighting glossy linoleum, gleaming countertops, shiny appliances.

"Jared and his family are going to love it. There are so many people who need this. If this works out, it could be a model for similar homes all over the nation. We'll invite the mayor, the governor, the state senators and representatives." Her eyes lit with enthusiasm. "Maybe the president will hear about it and —"

Sam held up a hand. He could see where she was heading. As usual, she took his breath away with her energy and vision.

She smiled sheepishly. "I was doing it

231

again, wasn't I? Running faster than I can walk."

"I love you for it. We'll find a way to share the community home with as many people as possible." He grabbed her hand. "Come on."

"Where are we going?"

"A quiet little spot I know of. The food's good, the music's soft, and the company is out of this world."

"It sounds too good to be true."

"Oh, it is," he promised.

"Just where is this dream place?"

"Not far from here."

"Did you make reservations?"

"We won't need them where we're going."

She tugged at his hand, pulling him to a stop. "Sam, I'm not taking another step until you tell me where we're going."

"Home. We're going home, sweetheart."

"Anyone ever tell you you're almost perfect?"

"Almost?"

"Well, you've still got to learn to make lasagna."

ABOUT THE AUTHOR

Jane McBride Choate has been weaving stories in her head ever since she can remember, but she shelved her dreams of writing to marry and start a family. After her third child was born, she wrote a short story and submitted it to a children's magazine. To her astonishment, it was accepted. Two children later, she is still creating stories. She believes in the healing power of love, which is why she writes romances. Jane and her husband, Larry, live with their five children in Loveland, Colorado.

Blessings in Disguise is Jane's sixth novel for AVALON, and the second in a series featuring Carla Stevens Hastings. The first book in the series, *Blessings of the Heart*, is now available from AVALON.

We hope you have enjoyed this Large Print book. Other Thorndike, Wheeler, and Chivers Press Large Print books are available at your library or directly from the publishers.

For information about current and upcoming titles, please call or write, without obligation, to:

Publisher
Thorndike Press
295 Kennedy Memorial Drive
Waterville, ME 04901
Tel. (800) 223-1244

or visit our Web site at:

www.gale.com/thorndike
www.gale.com/wheeler

OR

Chivers Large Print
published by BBC Audiobooks Ltd
St James House, The Square
Lower Bristol Road
Bath BA2 3SB
England
Tel. +44(0) 800 136919
email: bbcaudiobooks@bbc.co.uk
www.bbcaudiobooks.co.uk

All our Large Print titles are designed for easy reading, and all our books are made to last.